Sweet Poison

MARY FITT

With an introduction by Curtis Evans

 Moonstone Press

This edition published in 2024 by Moonstone Press
www.moonstonepress.co.uk

Introduction © 2024 Curtis Evans

Originally published in 1956 by Macdonald & Co, London.

Sweet Poison © the Estate of Kathleen Freeman, writing as Mary Fitt

The right of Kathleen Freeman to be identified as author of this work has been
asserted in accordance with the Copyright, Designs and Patents Act 1988

ISBN 978-1-899000-74-6
EISBN 978-1-899000-75-3

A CIP catalogue record for this book is available from the British Library

Text designed and typeset by Tetragon, London
Cover illustration by Jason Anscomb
Printed and bound by tk

Contents

INTRODUCTION

When *Sweet Poison* was published in 1956, it was author Kathleen Freeman's twenty-third Mary Fitt mystery novel in twenty years, an impressive rate of production indeed. Only three more Mary Fitt novels would follow before the author's untimely death in 1959 at the age of sixty-one. A final Fitt was posthumously published in 1960 and then the rest was silence, with Mary Fitt rarely appearing in print again until her revival over six decades later by Moonstone Press in 2022. *Sweet Poison* also was the penultimate Inspector Mallett and Dr. Fitzbrown detective novel, preceded in 1954 by *Love from Elizabeth* and followed in 1959 by *Mizmaze*, the investigative team's swansong. In tone, *Poison* strikes a balance between the serious character study of *Elizabeth* and the whimsy and seeming outright parody in *Mizmaze*: there is deliberate artificiality, dry humour and wit throughout *Poison*, but, at the same time, there are interesting points made therein about obsession with the past and the varied forms it can take. It was probably the most praised of the later Mary Fitt mystery novels, with, for example, Maurice Richardson in the *London Observer* exhorting: "Don't miss… Has a splendidly eccentric victim… Full of odd twists. One of Miss Fitt's most original capers." Not to be outdone, Francis Iles, aka Anthony Berkeley, a co-member with Fitt in the Detection Club, raved: "A really flavoursome dish for the gourmet of crime." More recently, in Jacques Barzun's and Wendell Hertig Taylor's *A*

Catalogue of Crime, the novel was lauded as a "deft mixture of poison and archaeology." I agree wholeheartedly with these enchanted reviewers. At around fifty thousand words, *Sweet Poison* makes a most refreshing light repast for classic mystery lovers.

Mary Fitt derived the title of *Sweet Poison* from one of the more obscure Shakespeare plays, *King John* ("Sweet, sweet, sweet poison for the age's tooth"). Back in 1930, when Dorothy L. Sayers published the first Lord Peter Wimsey mystery in which there appeared Lord Peter's future wife, Harriet Vane, Sayers titled the book *Strong Poison*, drawing this title from the traditional border ballad *Lord Randall*: "What did you have for your breakfast, my comfort and joy?/A cup of strong poison; mother, make my bed soon." English mystery writer Rupert Penny followed Sayers a decade later with *Sweet Poison* in 1940, a detective novel which literally concerns poisoned sweets and does not include the Shakespearean epigraph. Mary Fitt seems to have come next in 1956, followed by crime writers T. C. H. Jacobs (1966) and Douglas Clark (1970). In the last half-century, the phrase has become something of a hackneyed mystery title, but Mary Fitt came early and was the first to use the term in both literal and metaphorical senses (see below).

Appropriately for Kathleen Freeman, a distinguished classicist, her criminous alter ego Mary Fitt draws on the subject of excavated ancient Roman villas in Great Britain for the plot of *Sweet Poison*. The period of Roman control over the province of Britannia is traditionally dated from 43 to 410 AD. Rediscovered ruins of Roman villas have since been excavated in Britain for several hundred years, most recently just three years ago in the county of Rutland. In 1938 a local farmer discovered a Roman villa near the village of Low Ham in the county of Somerset while prosaically digging a hole to bury a dead sheep. During the Second World War the British government prohibited deep ploughing of the area, leaving excavation to be carried out between 1946 and 1955, the year Mary Fitt presumably wrote *Sweet Poison*. The Low Ham Roman Villa, as it is known, is famed for a large mosaic tile floor, lifted in 1953, depicting scenes from the lives of legendary lovers Dido and Aeneas. It has been called the earliest surviving piece of narrative art in Britain. Another excavated Roman villa, Chedworth Roman Villa, was discovered in 1864 by a gamekeeper digging for a live ferret. The broadminded and generous owner of the land, John Scott, the third Earl of Eldon, financed the resulting excavations as well as the construction of roofing for the elaborate mosaics and a mock-Tudor museum to house unearthed artifacts. Today Chedworth Roman Villa is a treasured historical monument.

In *Sweet Poison* Mary Fitt creatively imagines what might happen were a rather dottier—if not outright barmy—individual owned the land whereon precious Roman mosaics lay buried. In the novel a Roman villa is unearthed in Siccard, a small, rocky seaside resort, and a team of experts, including the novel's focal character Roger Royden, an archaeological chemist, descends to excavate it. The mosaics had been wonderfully preserved by a sandstorm which buried both the tiles and, tragically, the human inhabitants of the villa at the time. "These were mostly servants, animals and local women," the author observes sardonically, "so that the disaster hadn't mattered much at the time… But the archaeologists were not really interested in what happened to these obscure people some seventeen centuries ago; they were interested in the mosaics." Sadly for them, their effort to rescue, restore and preserve the mosaics in impeded by Augustus Gale, the imperious gentleman who owns neighbouring Geffrye House, a Georgian country mansion. On the grounds of Geffrye House part of the Roman villa—along with a section of its mosaics—lies buried.

Augustus refuses to allow his land to be dug up by the importunate archaeologists because he has an obsession with the past all his own which puts him in collision with the determined men of science. It seems that Geffrye House once was the home of noted Regency playwright Joan Farmer (1775–1817), who returned to the mansion to die after being deserted by her faithless actor husband. Once there stood a summer-house in the garden of Geffrye House (over a section of the Roman villa), making it sacred ground to Augustus, who has fallen, yes, madly in love with the dead woman. "It ought to be a national shrine," Augustus declares fervently, "but the nation which spends millions on football won't spare a few thousands for the preservation of its holy places."

In the grip of his overweening adoration of Joan Farmer, the infatuated man, as Maurice Richardson put it, "forces his family to live as if the clock had stopped in 1817." And the family, which includes Augustus' aged mother, adult son and daughter and a beautiful young second wife, Dulcibella, with whom Roger immediately becomes desperately smitten, are not too happy about this, to say the least. (There is also a much put-upon man-of-all-work named Robert Brooke.) Thus, there are plenty of people around at Geffrye House with reasons for wanting to see Augustus lying in the ground, just like those mosaics.

Readers of this introduction may have noticed that Joan Farmer's span of mortal years is identical to that of beloved real life English novelist Jane Austen, whose legions of devoted fans over the decades have been dubbed Janeites. Among male mystery writer contemporaries of Mary Fitt both American Rex Stout, creator of Nero Wolfe, and Anglo-American Richard Wilson

Webb, one-half of Patrick Quentin, were devoted admirers of Austen, Janeites if you will, and both men named Austen's *Emma* as their favourite novel. Although not a mystery novelist herself (though she parodied the Gothic mystery conventions in her novel *Northanger Abbey*), Jane Austen clearly influenced the manners school of mystery associated with the Golden Age Crime Queens Dorothy L. Sayers, Margery Allingham and Ngaio Marsh. A later Crime Queen, the late P. D. James, also was a great admirer of Austen and employed characters from *Pride and Prejudice* in her final detective novel, *Death Comes to Pemberley* (2011). Under her own name Kathleen Freeman published, the same year in which her manners mystery *Sweet Poison* appeared, *T'Other Miss Austen*, an admiring study of Jane Austen and her writing, which the website janeaustenbooks.net describes as a "witty bio ahead of its time in its treatment of Austen's particular genius." In the novel, however, Mary Fitt devilishly afflicts her characters with a privileged, deranged literary fanboy, or stan, who has crazily carried his fandom to the point of poisoning his own life and the lives of everyone around him. As such he makes an eminently worthy murder victim. But who actually does the dread deed? I leave that for you, dear readers, to discover for yourself, in this mordantly delightful and thought-provoking murder mystery.

ABOUT THE AUTHOR

One of the prominent authors of the classical detective fiction of the Golden Age and afterwards was herself a classicist: Kathleen Freeman, a British lecturer in Greek at the University College of South Wales and Monmouthshire, Cardiff (now Cardiff University) between 1919 and 1946. Primarily under the pseudonym Mary Fitt, Freeman published twenty-nine crime novels between 1936 and 1960, the last of them posthumously. Eighteen of these novels are chronicles of the criminal investigations of her series sleuth, Superintendent Mallett of Scotland Yard, while the remaining eleven of them, nine of them published under the pseudonym Mary Fitt and one apiece published under the respective names of Stuart Mary Wick and Kathleen Freeman, are stand-alone mysteries, some of which are notable precursors of the modern psychological crime novel. There is also a single collection of Superintendent Mallett 'cat mystery' short stories, *The Man Who Shot Birds*.

From the publication of her lauded debut detective novel, *Three Sisters Flew Home*, Mary Fitt—like Gladys Mitchell, an author with whom in England she for many years shared the distinguished publisher Michael Joseph—was deemed a crime writer for 'connoisseurs'. Within a few years, Fitt's first English publisher, Ivor Nicholson & Watson, proudly dubbed her devoted following a 'literary cult'. In what was an unusual action for the time, Nicholson & Watson placed on the dust jacket of their edition of Fitt's *Death at Dancing Stones* (1939) accolades from such distinguished, mystery-writing Fitt fans as Margery Allingham ('A fine detective story and a most ingenious puzzle'), Freeman Wills Crofts ('I should like to offer her my congratulations') and J. J. Connington ('This is the best book by Miss Mary Fitt I have yet read').

If not a crowned 'queen of crime' like Allingham, Agatha Christie, Dorothy L. Sayers and Ngaio Marsh, Kathleen Freeman in her Mary Fitt guise was, shall we say, a priestess of peccadillos. In 1950 Freeman was elected to the prestigious Detection Club, a year after her crime-writing cover was blown in the gossip column 'The Londoner's Diary' in the *Evening Standard*. Over the ensuing decade several of the older Mary Fitt mysteries were reprinted in paperback by Penguin and other publishers, while new ones continued to appear, to a chorus of praise from such keen critics of the crime-fiction genre as Edmund Crispin, Anthony Berkeley Cox (who wrote as, among others, Francis Iles) and Maurice Richardson. 'It is easy to run out of superlatives in writing of Mary Fitt,' declared the magazine *Queen*, 'who is without doubt among the first of our literary criminographers.'

Admittedly, Freeman enjoyed less success as a crime writer in the United States, where only ten of her twenty-nine mystery novels were published during her lifetime. However, one of Fitt's warmest boosters was the *New York Times*'s Anthony Boucher, for two decades the perceptive dean of American crime-fiction reviewers. In 1962, three years after Fitt's death, Boucher selected the author's 1950 novel *Pity for Pamela* for inclusion in the 'Collier Mystery Classics' series. In his introduction to the novel, Boucher lauded Fitt as an early and important exponent of psychological suspense in crime fiction.

Despite all the acclaim which the Mary Fitt mysteries formerly enjoyed, after Freeman's untimely death from congestive heart failure in 1959 at the age of sixty-one, the books, with very few exceptions—*Mizmaze* (Penguin, 1961), *Pity for Pamela* (Collier, 1962), *Death and the Pleasant Voices* (Dover, 1984)—fell almost entirely out of print. Therefore, this latest series of sparkling reissues from Moonstone is a welcome event indeed for lovers of vintage British mystery, of which Kathleen Freeman surely is one of the most beguiling practitioners.

*

A native Midlander, Kathleen Freeman was born at the parish of Yardley near Birmingham on 22 June 1897. The only child of Charles Henry Freeman and his wife Catherine Mawdesley, Kathleen grew up and would spend most of her adult life in Cardiff, where she moved with her parents not long after the turn of the century. Her father worked as a brewer's traveller, an occupation he had assumed possibly on account of an imperative need to support his mother and two unmarried sisters after the death of his own father, a schoolmaster and clergyman without a living who had passed away at the age of fifty-seven. This was in 1885, a dozen years before Kathleen was born, but presumably the elder Charles Freeman bequeathed a love of learning to his family, including his yet-unborn granddaughter. Catherine Mawdesley's father was James Mawdesley, of the English seaside resort town of Southport, not far from Liverpool. James had inherited his father's 'spacious and handsome silk mercer's and general draper's establishment', impressively gaslit and 'in no degree inferior, as to amplitude, variety and elegance of stock, to any similar establishment in the metropolis or inland towns' (in the words of an 1852 guide to Southport), yet he died at the age of thirty-five, leaving behind a widow and three young daughters.

As a teenager, Kathleen Freeman was educated at Cardiff High School, which, recalling the 1930s, the late memoirist Ron Warburton remembered as 'a large attractive building with a large schoolyard in front, which had a boundary wall between it and the pavement'. The girls attended classes on the ground floor, while the boys marched up to the first (respectively, the first and second floors in American terminology). 'The first-floor windows were frosted so that the boys could not look down at the girls in the school playground,' Warburton wryly recalled. During the years of the Great War, Freeman, who was apparently an autodidact in ancient Greek (a subject unavailable at Cardiff High School, although the boys learned Latin), attended the co-educational, 'red-brick' University College of South Wales and Monmouthshire, founded three decades earlier in 1883, whence she graduated with a BA in Classics in 1918. The next year saw both her mother's untimely passing at the age of fifty-two and her own appointment as a lecturer in Greek at her alma mater. In 1922, she received her MA; a Doctor of Letters belatedly followed eighteen years later, in recognition of her scholarly articles and 1926 book *The Work and Life of Solon*, about the ancient Athenian statesman. Between 1919 and 1926 Freeman was a junior colleague at University College of her former teacher Gilbert Norwood, who happened to share her great love of detective fiction, as did another prominent classical scholar, Gilbert Murray, who not long before his death in 1957 informed Freeman that he had long been a great admirer of Mary Fitt.

Freeman's rise in the field of higher education during the first half of the twentieth century is particularly impressive given the facts, which were then deemed disabling, of her sex and modest family background as the daughter of a brewer's traveller, which precluded the possibility of a prestigious Oxbridge education. 'A man will do much for a woman who is his friend, but to be suspected of being a brewer's traveller... was not pleasant,' observes the mortified narrator of William Black's novel *A Princess of Thule* (1883), anxious to correct this socially damning misimpression. Evidently unashamed of her circumstances, however, Freeman evinced a lifetime ambition to reach ordinary, everyday people with her work, eschewing perpetual confinement in academe's ivory tower.

Before turning to crime writing in 1936 under the alias of Mary Fitt, Freeman published five mainstream novels and a book of short stories, beginning with *Martin Hanner: A Comedy* (1926), a well-received academic novel about a (male) classics professor who teaches at a red-brick university in northern England. After the outbreak of the Second World War, while she was still employed at the university, Freeman, drawing on her classical education, published the patriotically themed *It Has All Happened Before: What the Greeks Thought of Their Nazis* (1941).* She also lectured British soldiers headed to the Mediterranean theatre of war on the terrain, customs and language of Greece, a country she had not merely read about but visited in the Thirties. During the cold war, when Freeman, passed over for promotion, had retired from teaching to devote herself to writing in a world confronted with yet another totalitarian menace, she returned to her inspirational theme, publishing *Fighting Words from the Greeks for Today's Struggle* (1952). Perhaps her most highly regarded layman-oriented work from this period is *Greek City-States* (1950), in which, notes scholar Eleanor Irwin, Freeman uses her 'uncanny eye for settings, as is often seen in her mysteries', to bring 'the city-states to life'. Freeman explicitly drew on her interests in both classicism and crime in her

---

* Under the heading of 'Dictators', Freeman quotes Solon: 'When a man has risen too high, it is not easy to check him after; now is the time to take heed of everything.' Timeless words indeed!

much-admired book *The Murder of Herodes and Other Trials from the Athenian Law Courts* (1946), which was effusively praised by the late Jacques Barzun, another distinguished academic mystery fancier, as 'a superb book for the [crime] connoisseur'.

In spite of her classical background, Kathleen Freeman derived her 'Mary Fitt' pseudonym—which she also employed to publish juvenile fiction, including a series of books about an intrepid young girl named Annabella—not from ancient Greece but from Elizabethan England, Eleanor Irwin has hypothesised, for the name bears resemblance to that of Mary Fitton, the English gentlewoman and maid of honour who is a candidate for the 'Dark Lady' of Shakespeare's queer-inflected sonnets. Irwin points out that Freeman's 'earliest literary publications were highly personal reflections on relationships in sonnet form'. The name also lends itself to a pun—'Miss Fitt'—which it is likely the author deliberately intended, given her droll wit and nonconformity.

While Kathleen Freeman's first four detective novels, which appeared in 1936 and 1937, are stand-alones, her fifth essay in the form, *Sky-Rocket* (1938), introduces her burly, pipe-smoking, green-eyed, red-moustached series police detective, Superintendent Mallett, who is somewhat reminiscent of Agatha Christie's occasional sleuth Superintendent Battle. The two men not only share similar builds but have similarly symbolic surnames.

Joined initially by acerbic police surgeon Dr. Jones and later by the imaginative Dr. Dudley 'Dodo' Fitzbrown—the latter of whom, introduced in *Expected Death* (1938), soon supersedes Jones— Superintendent Mallett would dominate Mary Fitt's mystery output over the next two decades. Only after Freeman's heart condition grew perilously grave in 1954 does it seem that the author's interest in Mallett and Fitzbrown dwindled, with the pair appearing in only two of the five novels published between 1956 and 1960. Similarly diminished in her final years was Freeman's involvement with the activities of the Detection Club, into which she initially had thrown herself with considerable zeal. In the first half of the decade she had attended club dinners with her beloved life partner, Dr. Liliane Marie Catherine Clopet, persuaded Welsh polymath Bertrand Russell, an omnivorous detective-fiction reader, to speak at one of the dinners, and wrote a BBC radio play, *A Death in the Blackout* (in which Dr. Fitzbrown appears), with the proceeds from the play going to the club.

Presumably Kathleen Freeman met Liliane Clopet at the University College of South Wales and Monmouthshire, where Clopet registered as a student in 1919. Precisely when the couple began cohabiting is unclear, but by 1929 Freeman had dedicated the first of what would be many books to Clopet ('For L.M.C.C.'), and by the Thirties the pair resided at Lark's Rise, the jointly owned house—including a surgery for Clopet and her patients—that the couple had built in St. Mellons, a Cardiff suburb. In the author's biography on the back of her Penguin mystery reprints, Freeman noted that a friend had described the home where she lived as 'your Italian-blue house', though she elaborated: 'It is not Italian, but it is blue—sky-blue.' There Freeman would pass away and Clopet would reside for many years afterwards.

Born on 13 December 1901 in Berwick-upon-Tweed in Northumberland, Liliane Clopet was one of three children of native Frenchman Aristide Bernard Clopet, a master mariner, and his English wife Charlotte Towerson, a farmer's daughter. Although Aristide became a naturalised British citizen, the Clopets maintained close connections with France. In 1942, during the Second World War, Liliane's only brother, Karl Victor Clopet—a master mariner like his father who for a dozen years had run a salvage tug in

French Morocco—was smuggled by Allied forces from Casablanca to London, where he provided details of Moroccan ports, beaches and coastal defences, which were crucially important to the victory of the United States over Vichy French forces at the ensuing Battle of Port Lyautey.

Even more heroically (albeit tragically), Liliane's cousin Evelyne Clopet served with the French Resistance and was executed by the Nazis in 1944, after British forces had parachuted her into France; at her death she was only twenty-two years old. In 1956, under another pseudonym (Caroline Cory), Kathleen Freeman published a novel set in wartime France, *Doctor Underground*, in which she drew on Evelyne's experiences. A couple of years earlier, Liliane Clopet herself had published a pseudonymous novel, *Doctor Dear*, in which she depicted a female physician's struggles with sexism among her colleagues and patients.

Kathleen Freeman, who was rather masculine-looking in both her youth and middle age (boyish in her twenties, she grew stouter over the years, wearing her hair short and donning heavy tweeds), produced no issue and at her death left her entire estate, valued at over £300,000 in today's money, to Liliane Clopet. In a letter to another correspondent she avowed: 'My books are my children and I love them dearly.' Admittedly, Freeman shared custody of her mysteries with that queer Miss Fitt, but surely she loved her criminally inclined offspring, too. I have no doubt that the author would be pleased to see these books back in print again after the passage of so many years. Readers of vintage mysteries, now eager to embrace the stylish and sophisticated country-house detective novels and psychological suspense tales of an earlier era, will doubtless be pleased as well.

CURTIS EVANS

Sweet Poison

"Sweet, sweet, sweet poison for the age's tooth."

SHAKESPEARE, *King John*, ACT I, SC. I

I

When Augustus Gale died of poison, all observers who knew him would have said, if they had known the truth as well as the idiom, that he had "asked for it".

Nobody said this or its equivalent because they all believed, except some of the immediate onlookers, that he had committed suicide. There were obvious reasons why he should have done this, and when the coroner recorded a verdict of "Suicide while the balance of his mind was disturbed", this was generally accepted, though most people who knew Augustus only superficially or by repute thought that the insanity was not temporary. This is the opinion held by all but a very few to this day.

But the truth is that Augustus was poisoned—got rid of like a rat—and that he had "asked for it". In order to understand how this came about, it is necessary to go back to that summer and show the first meeting between Roger Royden, an archæological chemist, and Dulcibella, Augustus's second wife.

2

Roger had come down to Siccard, which is a small seaside resort, with a group of excavators who needed his services. A Roman villa had been discovered in the neighbourhood, with wonderful mosaics under several feet of sand which had covered them in a sandstorm many centuries earlier, and so preserved them while burying the inhabitants. These were mostly servants, animals and local women, so that the disaster hadn't mattered much at the time; the owner, the rich Roman owner, had evidently been absent, and therefore there had not been any guests. This much the archæologists had already surmised, and each evening over dinner they were able to add something to their reconstruction. But they we not really interested in what had happened to these obscure people some seventeen centuries ago; they were interested in the mosaics.

The mosaics were truly remarkable. They were not only works of art such as had not before been discovered in Britain; they also threw light on the way of life of the Roman occupying forces during the second century after Christ. And it was certain that in due course, when they had been properly cleaned and restored, they would bring hosts of visitors to Siccard and a great deal of money, for they were not only important archæologically but of interest to the Common Man. It was thought that they would in fact rival the mosaics of Pompeii and Casale, and it was already being proposed in the Urban District Council that some of them should be permanently locked up—hidden from the eyes of ladies.

Difficulties of other kinds were arising for the archæologists; but let us postpone consideration of these while we watch Roger Royden coming in to dinner on a certain memorable evening, to join the party at the central table of Siccard's only good hotel, the Imperial.

3

The hotel was large and luxurious. The food was often quite good, and the service also. The archæologists would not have been there if they had not been a party and so been able to come to a favourable arrangement with the management. The hotel could hardly have survived if it had not been for the occasional windfalls like this; for normally it was uninhabited except for Easter, Whitsun and the two months of July and August.

It overlooked the wild sea, the glorious rocky coast, and unspoilt bleak country for many miles around; so that for the ordinary visitor there was nothing to do. Even bathing was prohibited; it was obviously dangerous, and often those who defied the prohibition lost their lives. Riding, motoring, golf, all were difficult or impossible. There was nothing to do at Siccard, except walk along the soft turf of the cliffs when it wasn't too windy, or stare out from the hotel windows at the waves crashing on the rocks, and wonder why anybody ever came here, to live or to stay.

Yet history clung to the place and eddied round it: tragic stories of shipwrecks and lost loves and far-off battles and ghosts, such as had appealed to nineteenth-century novelists but which have no appeal now.

The seagulls were happier, rearing families on the high ledges where no one could disturb them, and waiting for the tides to bring them their food. But their joyous cries added to the melancholy of the place.

4

On this memorable evening Roger, as he reached the seat the head waiter pulled out for him at the central table, glanced first over his left shoulder to see if she was there.

She was.

He gave a start, for he had not expected her. Every Friday evening he schooled himself not to expect her—to be disappointed as one always must be in "real" life—and every Friday she was there.

The dining-room at the Imperial Hotel—so called because the Kaiser had once stayed there for a night—was divided into two unequal parts. The main section was on a slightly lower level than the rest, which was like a stage raised one step above the restaurant proper; this upper stage had only half a dozen tables and these though seldom occupied were adorned and made to look special by chosen flowers. This part of the dining-room always looked as if it were waiting for distinguished guests who never came—except on Fridays.

Every Friday evening there was this one guest: a woman, youngish, not too young, with smooth black hair parted in the middle. She wore jewels, usually diamonds and she was always in full evening dress as if she expected to be joined by someone. But though she looked towards the entrance she was never joined by anyone. She was always alone.

She came in before the archæological party, by the time Roger entered late, she had finished her meal and was smoking over coffee and a liqueur. Roger wondered if she ever ate anything, because the archæologists came as soon as the gong sounded and ate faster than anyone— they simply lowered their shoulders and devoured the food put before them, their appetites sharpened by the day's work in the open air—yet they were only halfway through dinner when he arrived and she was already served with her usual coffee and liqueur.

Roger felt an intense curiosity about her—his colleagues felt none. He wished to know what liqueur she drank: the golden liquid was probably Benedictine. The coffee was black: they saw her wave away the waiter's attempt to pour simultaneously from two pots. Above all, where did she come from? And why did she come here, alone, every Friday, to dine?

As he glanced at her, as usual, over his left shoulder, she gave him a slight sign of acknowledgment. It was not a smile nor an inclination of the head; just the slightest change of expression. He received it, offered a bow which was not returned, and took his place.

No one had noticed this exchange; yet it was this that made the evening memorable.

5

The wolfish appetites of the archæologists made it possible for Roger to outstay them. Before he had finished his soup they had all flung down their table-napkins and rushed out.

When the head waiter came to ask Roger what he wanted next, Roger motioned to him to lean down. Then he said:

"Who is that lady on the dais?"

Roger spoke low and she could not possibly have heard him, yet he was convinced that she would know of his inquiry. The waiter said:

"That's Mrs. Augustus Gale from Geffrye House."

Roger indicated that he would like fish. This was not true; he detested fish as served by the Imperial Hotel, but he wanted something that could be eaten quickly and his only fear was lest the lady on the dais should vanish for another week. He was glad to hear that she was married: this made it possible for him to approach her later, if she stayed long enough. Roger had been brought up by a Victorian mother and he would have thought it improper to approach without introduction any unmarried girl, and a little risky too.

He swallowed the fish, making light of a few bones, and then rose. He crossed the room and stepped on to the dais. He heard himself saying in a hollow voice:

"May I ask the waiter to bring my coffee here?"

"Of course," said the lady in answer to this preposterous suggestion.

"Excuse me," said Roger belatedly, "if I force my company on you. My name is Roger Royden and I am attached to the archæo-logical party that is—"

"I know," said the lady. "Do sit down."

The waiter brought Roger's coffee to the table, and he asked the lady to have some more, which she declined, or another liqueur, which she accepted, and Roger at last had the pleasure of knowing that she was indeed drinking Benedictine.

"It is nice of you," said the lady, "to join me. It is boring to dine alone."

Roger did not know what to say to this: so many thoughts suggested themselves to him that he could not choose one of them to express. None of them seemed worth expressing, anyway. He decided to launch a new subject.

"You are Mrs. Gale?"

"Yes." She could put more expression into a monosyllable than most people can into a speech. "I am Mrs. *Augustus* Gale."

"I do not know your husband—"

"No."

"But I know *of* him."

"I'm sure you do. He has interfered with your plans. He likes to interfere with plans."

Roger looked up. There was no bitterness in her tone, but there was a tinge of malice, and she was smiling.

"Not *my* plans," he said gently. "The plans of my colleagues, perhaps." He now felt composed enough to look at her steadily. She was handsome: her skin was pale and thick, like a magnolia petal, but this appearance might have been due to a thick make-up. Her lips were very red. Her eyes were large and dark blue, and her eyebrows were as black as her hair. She wore some pervasive scent. He added: "Is there any chance that he will change his mind?"

"Not the slightest," said Mrs. Gale. "Augustus never changes his mind if this would convenience people. Tell me," she said, leaning her elbows on the table and her chin, which was round with a dimple in it, on her hands, "is there a verb 'to convenience'?—the opposite of 'to inconvenience', I mean?"

"I don't think so," said Roger, put out by her approximation and the look of deep interest which accompanied it. "I think the verb would be 'to oblige'."

"Oh, one can't say that!" cried she. "Only charwomen 'oblige'! But never mind: the point is, Augustus knows he is inconveniencing a great many people, and he is enjoying this. He will not change his mind. What will you do?"

"I?" said Roger. "It has nothing to do with me. My colleagues are discussing possible steps." He spoke stiffly because her manner suggested that she was in sympathy with her husband in his attitude. The position was, from the archæologists' point of view, serious. The Roman villa they were excavating happened to be partly on Augustus Gale's land, or rather Geffrye House, an eighteenth-century mansion built on the site of an old farm-house, happened to straddle in part over the Roman mosaics. The wall of Geffrye House ran across a corner of the Roman villa and so enclosed a most interesting area of mosaic in Augustus Gale's garden. The archæologists had asked permission to continue their work on the other side of the wall; Augustus Gale had refused.

Representations had been made to him, but without result. The archæologists were wondering if they, with the support of the Urban District Council, could apply to the Minister of Works for some compulsory powers, but they were afraid to bring this siege-engine up to the walls lest it should be ineffectual, for then they would have destroyed all chances of peaceful negotiations with the owner. This topic had formed the sole subject of discussion, apart from the occasional discovery of a fibula or a sesterce, for the last week, and Roger was sick of it. He knew they were all discussing it now in the smoke-room.

"There are no possible steps," said the lady, "that could compel Augustus. He has already consulted his lawyers: he will stand on his rights as a property owner and he will take the case to the House of Lords if necessary." Again there was the note of triumph, or pride, or whatever it was.

"How silly!" said Roger.

"Why silly? If it is what he wants—"

"But it will cost so much!"

"Augustus does not mind paying for what he wants—but you are angry with me. You think I am on Augustus's side."

"That would be natural," said Roger mildly.

"No," said the lady with sudden vehemence, "it would *not* be natural. I would like you—or your friends—to win. I will even suggest a possible way—the only possible way."

"Really?" said Roger.

"Yes. I suggest you come and stay in our house. I invite you. You will be a Trojan Horse."

"But what could I do?"

"Make friends with Augustus. Do you know anything about the Regency period?"

"Yes, I think so."

"Then that is all you need. Come tomorrow." She rose.

"But—" said Roger.

"You mean, what is there to pay? I'll be frank with you. I have a daughter; she needs a husband."

"You—a daughter of marriageable age?" The flattery was gross but unconscious. She smiled:

"My stepdaughter, Cornelia. I am Dulcibella. I am Augustus's second wife."

"Of course." Roger stared at her. "But I could not possibly come on *those* terms."

"I don't mean *you* are to marry her, silly creature!" said Dulcibella. "I am not as crude as that! I mean, when you have got round Augustus—which you will easily do: I have been watching you and I know—you will then introduce your colleagues—the young unmarried ones: Cornelia is not much over twenty—into the house. One of them will fall in love with her. You may do so yourself: she is very pretty."

"Oh no!" said Roger fervently.

She smiled. "Now you know your part. Come and dine tomorrow. Be well primed in the history of Geffrye House—you know it, of course?"

"Roughly."

"Well, know it smoothly and well. Augustus will ask you to stay. You will agree."

"Thank you."

She swept out, leaving scent behind her, and an indelible impression on Roger's heart, which before had been only slightly scratched: the "heart", of course, is here symbolically used to represent his emotional life only a microscope, or an infra-red apparatus, to continue the metaphor, could have detected the earlier scratches; but Dulcibella had made a deep mark like a cuneiform sign.

Roger was discomfited, though he did not yet know the cause.

6

He was discomfited, too, when late that night a note was brought to him on a salver.

He was sitting with his colleagues on the veranda of the hotel. The evening was warm—it was May—and on the opposite coast a lighthouse blinked reliably at half-second intervals—one, two, three and an occultation of eight and a half seconds. The archæologists were talking desultorily about the day's work, which had not been very profitable: a great amount of sand had been sifted, a small portion, about a foot square, of the *tesserae* had been uncovered. They were not disappointed: archæology requires long and patient work to achieve its results, which at the time are apt to seem unsensational. Roger listened: he did not come into this, for there had been nothing for him to do. When the waiter stood beside him and held out the salver, Roger's heart—his physical heart this time—leapt. He took the note, tore open the envelope with forced deliberation and in confident expectation of a disappointment. It said:

"I forgot to tell you that we dine at five." It was unsigned.

"What, notes already?" said someone, and there was a laugh.

"I am—dining there tomorrow," said Roger.

"Whew!"

Roger disliked them. He decided to go to bed. As he walked off, he heard a quick step behind him. He turned to see the leader of the expedition, a tall, red-haired, stooping man called Riley.

"I say." Roger stopped, unwillingly. "Is it *true* you are dining with the Gales? Then—you'll see what you can do for the Expedition, won't you? Praa climbed up on to the wall this morning early before anyone was about, and he says the old fool has begun to remove the sand. He has made a deep pit. The *tesserae* are already coming unstuck. The whole thing is sagging in the middle. If it's to be saved it'll need careful treatment."

"Well, what can I do?" protested Roger.

"Explain to the old boy that if he leaves it exposed it will be destroyed by the weather: heavy rain or frost. Tell him the only reason it's been preserved till now is that the sand has covered it. You'll do that?"

"I'll try, if I get an opening."

"Have you ever met Gale?"

"No."

"Only his wife?"

"Only Mrs. Gale."

"So it was she who invited you?" said Riley, with an inflection of the voice which made Roger want to knock him down.

"Yes."

"I'm glad you're going."

Roger did not reply. He hated being regarded by them as a Trojan Horse, whatever Dulcibella might have said. He had been thinking over all that she had said, and he had decided that next time, with her permission, he would take along one other man as a possible suitor for Cornelia. The man he had in mind was his friend Martin Praa, a fat, blond, pleasant fellow five or six years younger than himself, and obviously in the state of mind of a man looking for a wife.

Roger was eager to please Mrs. Gale, and to further her very laudable wish to marry off her stepdaughter Cornelia. It did not occur to him that Cornelia should be consulted; he gave her no thought at that time. He was to make amends for this later.

"Well, if you won't help," he heard Riley saying, "it's too bad; but I should have thought that *esprit de corps*… By the way, it might help if you could flatter the old boy by knowing something about the house. Geffrye House has quite a history, you know. Would you like to borrow…?" He named two or three books, including the county guide.

"I should, thank you," said Roger with surprising alacrity.

Riley ran to his room to get the books. Roger spent half the night reading them. This was not a waste of the night hours, because he could not have slept, anyway. But since his mind was not fixed on what he read, he retained little. The accounts differed, and the one piece of information they had in common was something he knew already, namely that a young woman called Joan Farmer had lived there: she had written several plays which had been performed on the London stage in the first decade of the nineteenth century; she had achieved considerable fame, or notoriety, had married an actor, had been deserted by him, and had come home to Geffrye House to die.

Even in this story the accounts did not agree; but they were all sure, especially the county guide, that the ghost of Joan Farmer was one of the sights of the place.

Roger primed himself with the facts and surmises about Joan Farmer, and even managed to learn her dates, 1775 to 1817, before he fell asleep.

II

Roger had no car. He rode about on a Vespa, which was economical to run and easy to park.

He dressed with care, but he assumed that it would be right to wear a dark suit: no one could expect him to put on a dinner-jacket in the afternoon.

When he reached the enormous front gates of Geffrye House he found them shut. They were wrought-iron gates hung on square stone pillars each surmounted by an odd-looking heraldic bird, possibly a griffin. There were side gates for pedestrians; one of these was open.

He manœuvred the Vespa into position so that he could ride through this smaller gate: the drive was long and newly covered with ochre-coloured gravel. A loud voice from nearby stopped him. He looked up. A man was standing on the inner side of the gates.

"Sorry, you can't bring that thing in here," said the man.

"Why not?" said Roger, reddening. Like all people unused to commanding, he resented any opposition. "I am here at the invitation of—Mrs. Gale."

The man shook his head.

"The small gate is for those on foot. And I can't open the big gates to motor-traffic. The Boss doesn't allow it. Only carriages, see? Gentlemen's carriages, not tradesmen." He poked his red face through the bars of the gates: "Leave the Vespa there, sir, and walk. It won't hurt you. I'll take care of the machine, never fear."

Roger gave way. He pushed the Vespa through the gate, feeling silly and hoping that no one could see him from the many-windowed house. The lodge-keeper said:

"That's right, sir. You one of them archæologists?"

"Yes."

"Then this is your first visit. You want to be careful."

"In what way?"

"Fall in with the Boss's ways. Humour him. You may think he's mad and this is a loony-bin—at first. I know I did. But don't worry: when you get your eye in it's all right. Just humour him, see?" He went off, pushing the Vespa up the shallow steps into the lodge. "We're going to have a storm. But your bike'll be all right in here."

Roger set off up the yellow-ochre drive, trying to keep his well-shone shoes clean. There was a fresh wind blowing. The tide was coming in, and he could hear its preliminary crashings on the rocky edge of the shore, and the rumbling as the waves succeeded, dragging down the stones with them.

The front of the huge house showed no sign of life. It seemed to him, as he approached, that all the curtains were drawn. This was odd, because it was daylight, and the sun was still far from setting. Besides, the porch towards which he was making was on the north side, so that there could never be any need to shield these windows from the rays of the sun.

Roger felt awkward as soon as he stepped into the house. To begin with, he had only a beret to hand to the manservant who opened the door. It was a large beret, which he always wore when riding the Vespa, but in the hands of his attendant it looked ludicrous, and the man clearly did not know what to do with it. Roger did not offer to solve the problem.

In a moment he was shown into a room full of talking people. The room was dim and at first he thought it was lighted by candles; but when his eyes refocused themselves he saw that the light came from a ceiling chandelier; the chandelier itself was antique, made of hundreds of crystals, but the lighting was electric—dim and yellow, like candlepower. The contrast with the brilliant daylight outside was notable; Roger saw that, as he had thought, the heavy curtains were drawn.

Dulcibella detached herself from a small group near the fireplace and came towards him. She and all the other women—the company seemed to be mostly women —were in dinner dress.

"I am so glad you came. I want to introduce you to my husband. Augustus, this is Mr. Royden."

The man who stepped out of the group was shorter than Roger, strongly built and dark—very dark. The impression of darkness—black hair growing up in a peak from his forehead and left rather long, thick black eyebrows—was accentuated by the fact that he had let his hair grow down his cheek in long side-whiskers, wedge-shaped hair clipped short. Also he wore a loosely fitting, long-tailed dark coat, and a very large dark cravat. He held out a thick small hand the back of which was covered with black hairs.

Roger was then presented, by Augustus, to "my mother". Mrs. Gale, senior, seemed almost as broad as she was high; but this did not appear to be due to obesity but to some kind of shortening, as though she had been pressed nearer to the ground by a weight on her head. Even her face seemed like the widened version of another face, as if seen in a distorting mirror. Her face was white, her hair was shining white, her small soft hand was yellowish-white. She

smiled the thin wide smile of a toad as she took Roger's hand in
both hers. He was then presented to "my daughter Cornelia". He
looked with interest at the girl proposed by her stepmother for
marriage: she was tall—taller than her father—and moderately
pretty, with brown hair and parted lips. Her only notable features
were her eyes, which were bright blue, and her dress, which
Roger observed as odd, though he could not have described it. If
he had tried he might have said it was a bit like a nightdress; but
this would not have conveyed much, because Roger's knowledge
of women's nightwear was minimal. He would not have tried to
describe Cornelia's appearance because he had the fixed idea that
men don't notice such things; but he did notice it, and if he had
been willing to try to describe it—for the sake of a prospective
suitor, Martin Praa for instance—he would have said that it was
sort of high-waisted, of the style he believed to be Empire. But he
would have been wrong: Cornelia's dress was not of the style called
Empire, though it was high-waisted. All the ladies wore long gloves.

One or two other introductions and presentations were made
before dinner was announced. Rupert Gale, a young, taller version
of Cornelia, very bored-looking; an old professor whose name he
didn't catch, who seemed to want to take him into a corner and bore
him but who was prevented, several times, by Dulcibella; a couple
of young children, presumably of the second marriage, who were
brought in by a tutor and a governess and quickly removed; and an
unidentified young woman called Miss Smith, who, he learnt later,
was Augustus's "helper", a sort of combination of secretary and
looker-up of references and so on. There was no smoking during
this preliminary assembly, and no drinks were served. There was
no chance to talk to anyone because quite soon after his arrival
dinner was announced.

He glanced, first at the clock on the mantelpiece, then surreptitiously at his wristwatch. It was one minute to five.

2

At dinner he sat on Dulcibella's right hand; next to him on his right hand was Cornelia.

The light was so dim here that it was some time before he began to be aware of the other diners; when he looked up he saw that in this room the only lighting was by candles in sconces on the walls, and in one candelabra in the centre of the long table. He became aware that his noticing that there were more women than men was a delusion; there were five of each. The illusion was created by the fact that the women were all dressed in the same kind of dress as Cornelia, so that they were conspicuous. There seemed to be no one present except members of the family: Augustus, his mother, his son and daughter, and Dulcibella, as well as a middle-aged married pair whom Roger never identified but who seemed to be relatives. There was also, on Augustus's left hand, his secretary, Miss Smith; and there was the Professor. Otherwise Roger was the only outsider, and very much of an outsider he felt. He would have felt more so had he not been aware of Dulcibella's attention; she seemed apart from the family, too, and after all he was her guest, not Augustus's, really.

Cornelia broke into a conversation between him and Dulcibella by saying:

"You are an archæologist?"

"Well, not exactly," said Roger.

"I thought you were with the party who are investigating some Roman remains outside our wall?"

"Yes. But I am only attached to the party. Every archæological expedition needs consultants in other fields. I am what is called a chemist." Roger was used to being misunderstood when he said this, so he went on to explain —for he did not want to be misunderstood by Dulcibella, who was listening: "That is, not a pharmaceutical chemist, but an analytical chemist: one who analyses substances and describes, if possible, their chemical composition."

"I see," said Cornelia slowly, crumbling her bread. "And is there much for you to do?"

"Sometimes. I don't suppose you know that our work is becoming more and more necessary for dating specimens as well as describing them. It was chemical analysis that revealed the Piltdown skull as a forgery."

The other diners broke off their conversations to listen. Roger, embarrassed as always by attention, stopped.

"Do go on," said Dulcibella with a peculiar smile; he felt that she was challenging, even baiting him; he responded to the challenge.

"My principal work," he said, "is to preserve things the others dig up. Some things, like wood, have to be left moist, others have to be treated in some way until they reach a museum. One has to know the correct method to apply to each substance, including bones."

"Ah yes," said Dulcibella. "Tell us about bones. Bones are so interesting, I think. I often sit and look at people and wonder about their bones. I even strip them of their flesh—"

"My dear!" admonished Augustus.

"But I *do*, Augustus," said Dulcibella. "Now *you* have a wonderful skull. My skull is small and I'm sure, mean-looking. I shall never see it."

"You could," said Roger eagerly. "X-ray—"

"No, thank you," said Dulcibella. "Make the offer to Cornelia: she has her father's bones and her skull would not disgrace her."

Roger grew pink, not knowing what to say and aware that Dulcibella was teasing him. Luckily the Professor piped out:

"What was that you said about the Piltdown skull?"

"I was referring, sir, to the recent discovery."

"What recent discovery? The Piltdown skull was found in 1912."

"The discovery that it was a forgery, or rather, that the jaw was 'planted' so as to be associated with a Pleistocene skull-cap. This was finally established by a chemical test—the fluorine test—"

Roger was now launched and, egged on by Dulcibella, and also by Cornelia, he would have proceeded to explain to the table what was meant by the fluorine test, when the Professor said angrily:

"Young man, you are over-credulous! You accept the latest theory. I can assure you I knew Dawson personally, and he was incapable of the scandalous deception you speak of."

"Sir," said Roger, "I said nothing about Dawson. He may have been equally deceived by the forger if it was not he. All I said was, the two portions of the Piltdown skull, so-called, don't belong together, and this was demonstrated, after suspicion was aroused, by the fluorine test. The same test has been, and is being, applied to other supposed palæolithic skeletons."

The Professor was scarlet with rage. His white beard moved up and down but no sound issued from his lips.

"I grant you," said Roger courteously, "that as a method of accurate dating the fluorine test is inadequate. Unless there is a gap of, let us say, ten thousand years—"

Everybody laughed. The Professor sank back, appeased. Dulcibella rose, and the ladies left.

The Professor stayed to drink one glass of port, and after a few inarticulate mumblings, left without apology. Augustus said to the other two:

"Will you please leave us? I wish to have a talk with Mr. Royden before we rejoin the ladies."

"Here it comes!" thought Roger. He turned to face the enemy who was sitting back in his chair with both his hairy fists on the table.

Augustus was watching Roger with a smile.

3

Roger said: "I beg your pardon?" as if Augustus had spoken.

"I did not speak," said Augustus.

"You looked as though you were about to say something."

"I was not about to say anything."

"You looked as though you were thinking—"

"Of course I was thinking," said Augustus. "Unfortunately one cannot stop. But I am not in the habit of speaking my thoughts aloud. Still, if I take that line, conversation will cease, and as I am your host I must not allow that to happen. I will ask you a question: why have you come here?"

Roger was startled. Was this very disconcerting man about to accuse him of an interest in his wife? He said cautiously:

"I came because I was invited."

"Do you always accept invitations?" said Augustus.

"Usually, if there is no reason why I should not."

"You would have done better not to accept this one. Could you not see any reason why you should refuse it?"

Roger wished to smoke. His hand went to his breast pocket where was his cigarette case, but something prevented him from following the movement through. For one thing, there was no sign that Augustus intended to smoke. There were no cigarettes or cigars visible, nor any ash-trays.

"I suppose," said Roger slowly, "you are referring to the difference of opinion between you and the archæological party?"

"Difference of opinion!" Augustus scowled. "It is more than that. It is war. If any of your people tries to set foot on my property, I will shoot him!"

"You can't do that."

"You mean, I can't do it with impunity. Anyone can do anything, even in these times, if he is willing to accept the consequences."

"True," said Roger. "I hadn't thought of that." He remembered his duty to his colleagues and said mildly: "May I ask why you have such a fixed antagonism to the party? They are only doing their job, a perfectly harmless one."

"Harmless! When they mean to destroy—"

"Surely not," said Roger. "*They* aren't out to destroy anything; they want to preserve something."

"They have all they need outside my wall."

"They want to make a complete study of this mosaic pavement—unique in this country."

"They can never do that. My wall runs over part of it."

"The mosaic must run under the wall, intact. We've taken soundings. The wall has a foundation four feet under the sod. The mosaic was covered with eight feet of sand and clay on which there had accumulated some two feet of soil, grass-grown. Presumably those who built your boundary-wall were unaware—"

"I know all that," snapped Augustus. "I have taken my own

soundings. I have uncovered enough of the mosaic on my side of the wall to satisfy myself that it is not worth uncovering the rest."

"You mean," said Roger, "you'll cover it up again? That's a good idea, if you don't intend to let us take a look at it. At least that would preserve it. But why do you say it's not worth uncovering the rest?"

Augustus withdrew his clenched hands from the table, and regarded Roger with a smile that was now rather pitying than hostile.

"My dear young man, I see you are ignorant of the history, the true value, of this ground. It is, to me at any rate, holy ground, and it ought to be to all men of sensibility. It was in a summer-house built against that wall on a hillock which, curiously enough, was above the mosaic, that an incomparable woman—a woman of genius—wrote her last and one of her greatest works. Never"—he struck the table—"never will I allow that shrine to be disturbed! I would not do so if there were buried treasure—gold—instead of a few crude Roman mosaics. But this ignorant generation—"

Roger stared at him in astonishment. Augustus had gone red with anger and veins had swelled up in his neck and forehead.

"Do you mean," said Roger quietly, "Joan Farmer?"

4

Augustus appeared to relax.

"I do not expect you—or your colleagues—to understand my attitude. It is one that is quite foreign to this age and generation. People work for what the Germans call *realien*, not the things of the mind. They want bones, treasure, *mosaics*." He hissed the last word. "The spiritual significance of everything is lost upon them. Young man"—he leaned forward as if threateningly—"do you know why I bought this property?"

"I can guess—now," said Roger, aware that no answer was needed or would be listened to.

"I bought it," said Augustus, "because it was falling down. A strange reason, is it not"—he smiled again—"in this materialistic age?"

Roger bowed: he found himself beginning to be swayed by the atmosphere of the place, and by what was expected of him.

"Not so strange, if you consider it, as I do, a shrine. It ought to be a national shrine, but the nation which spends millions on football won't spare a few thousands for the preservation of its holy places. There was then no Joan Farmer Society, to do what has been done at Haworth and even Chawton—God knows that is little enough. So, sir, it has been my inspiration and my lifework to do what no one else has thought of: to preserve, as my worthless contemporaries won't do, a treasure for a possibly—probably—equally worthless posterity."

"You take a dim view, sir, of the human race."

"They offer me no opportunity to do otherwise. Still, their stupidity and lack of the power of valuation enabled me to fulfil my desire. I was able to buy this property for a sum within my means. And, sir, I will defend it against all-comers."

Roger reflected. After a while, he said:

"Sir, is no compromise possible between these conflicting points of view?"

"On my side, there can be no compromise. I will not allow your wretched diggers to interfere with my plans. It is a great misfortune that these miserable mosaics have been unearthed."

"What I meant was," said Roger patiently, "I feel sure that my colleagues, if they heard your reasons for refusing them admission, would understand. Would you consent to see the leader of the expedition and have a discussion?"

"I doubt," said Augustus, "if any solution can be reached. But I will not refuse to hear what your friends have to say. Bring them here—bring them here." He leaned forward in his fierce-looking way: "Are you staying here overnight?"

"No, sir," said Roger.

"Why not?"

"I was not invited to do so. I was invited to dine."

"Then I invite you to come tomorrow se'nnight and bring two of your friends. Only two: the table does not allow of more, nor do the resources of our kitchen, alas!"

Roger remembered that "se'nnight" was short for "seven-night" and meant "in a week's time". He bowed.

"I will inform my wife and daughter," said Augustus. "I shall expect you. It should be amusing for me. Your feeble arguments will amuse me. I like to be amused." He spoke less harshly. "When you do me the pleasure of spending the night here I will show you my collection. And now I think we will join the ladies."

He rose.

5

As, stiff-backed, Augustus led the way out of the room. Roger focused his eyes on the middle of the shoulders in front of him. Was he mistaken? No, the coat was undoubtedly blue, not black. Certainly Augustus's dress was odd in several ways.

Augustus turned suddenly:

"What are you staring at?"

"Nothing," said Roger.

"Young man, you are not called upon to criticise my ways nor the ways of my household. I do as I please, I run this house as I please. Do not imagine that you can interfere."

"I never thought of it," said Roger truly.

"Good. Follow me." Augustus seemed to be appeased, but there was something in his manner that alarmed Roger. He was glad to be released from the tête-à-tête and to find himself in the drawing-room with the others. The same atmosphere prevailed here under the dim light of the huge crystal chandelier, but it did not seem so thickly concentrated.

Roger sat down beside a lady in a yellow dress whom he thought to be Dulcibella. When she turned and he saw it was Cornelia he started with surprise.

6

"I'm sorry to disappoint you," said Cornelia with a perspicacious smile.

"Please!" said Roger, not knowing what to say.

"Please what?" said Cornelia, challengingly.

"Please don't put me in such an awkward position. I have not deserved it. Besides, I hate it when people pretend to read my thoughts. Don't you?"

"That depends," said Cornelia. "Sometimes I like it. Sometimes I wish they could really read my thoughts."

"Why?"

"Because they might be frightened into *doing* something."

"About what?" Roger was lost.

"About me, of course! Nothing else interests me."

"You are frank. But I don't believe you. You must be interested in many other things—and people. We all are."

"Yes," said Cornelia, bringing out a small fan and moving it slowly while she gazed at him over the top of it. "But I am interested only in so far as they affect *me*. I admit it; others would not."

"I see," said Roger lamely. Like other people, when he said "I see" it usually meant that he was quite lost. He was also thinking that Cornelia had the most brilliant-blue eyes it was possible to have and that the pupils were black, and the eyelashes very long and black, and the whole effect was most pleasing, and that Cornelia was flirting with him. He glanced round hastily, afraid, as always, of ridicule, but could not see that anyone was taking the slightest notice of them.

"Have you," said Cornelia brightly, "been worrying my father about the mosaic? I hope not: it will make him even more intolerable than usual."

Roger said mechanically, "You can't be more or less intolerable: you are either tolerable or you are not."

"Rubbish!" said Cornelia tartly. "Grammatically you are of course correct, my dear professor."

"I'm not a professor," said Roger. "I'm—"

"I know." She waved aside his explanation with her fan. "But you will be if you look at things in that way."

"In what way?"

"So pedantically. You say Daddy can't be more or less intolerable. I say he can—in this sense. Daddy is always intolerable—but sometimes he is intolerable in an ordinary way, a way we're all used to, and then something happens that makes him so intolerable that we can't bear to be near him, even. *Now* do you understand?"

"I *think* so," said Roger, enjoying being surprised at every turn of the conversation.

"You didn't answer my question. Have you been talking to him about the mosaic?"

"A little. But not enough to enrage him. In fact, he asked me to stay the night."

"And you accepted?" said Cornelia with unconcealed eagerness.

"No."

"Oh dear! Why not?"

"I have work to do tomorrow. Besides, I'd have to get my things from the hotel."

"How formal and conventional you are! Surely it wouldn't matter if you slept in your skin for one night?"

Roger was rather shocked at this: in his view young ladies did not think of naked men, nor even of men in pyjamas. He looked sullen and obstinate: he thought he knew she was trying to shock him, to make him look priggish and professional, and he would not play by explaining to her that he must have also a razor and a toothbrush.

"In this house," said Cornelia happily, "it could be a recommendation."

Roger's skin prickled. What sort of a house had he stepped into? Were they all mad, or was Cornelia hinting that he was here for an unlawful purpose?

"You *must* stay," she went on. "I can't bear it if you don't. I will get you all the paraphernalia you need: I'll borrow."

"That's all right, thank you," said Roger; and to gain time and release, he added: "Your father has allowed me to put off my visit until today se'nnight—"

"You *do* know that means a week, not a fortnight?" interrupted Cornelia. "Forgive me—of course you do. But in the past our visitors have got it wrong. Daddy forgets they don't know the expression and then when they don't turn up he gets madly angry, and when at last they do he throws them out. I don't want that to happen to you."

"It won't. He asked me to bring two other members of the party."

"And will you?"

"Of course. I shall bring the leader of our expedition, a chap called Riley, and my friend Martin Praa. You'll like Praa; he is a very good draughtsman."

"And why," said Cornelia with one of her mocking smiles, "should I be specially interested in a draughtsman? I don't want a man to draw me. I want—" She stopped.

Roger was afraid to ask "What?" for fear lest she told him. There was a lull in the conversation throughout the room, and it is always in such lulls that the most embarrassing remarks seem to be made. He was relieved to see Dulcibella coming towards them. He stood up.

7

Dulcibella also carried a fan. The eyes that gazed up at him over the top of it were black and provocative.

"What's this I hear?" she said.

"I don't know," said Roger, unable to imagine what Augustus had thought fit to report to her.

"My husband has asked you to spend tonight here," said Dulcie gravely, "and you have refused."

"No, I haven't *refused*, " said Roger, "I merely didn't accept."

"Oh well, I can second the invitation—and you can't refuse *me* anything. Now can you?"

Cornelia said with a giggle: "He feels he must have the protection of pyjamas."

"Really?" said Dulcibella, unruffled. "There are no pyjamas in this house; but I could lend you one of Augustus's nightshirts."

"God!" muttered Roger.

"It would be a bit short on *you*," said Dulcibella, eyeing his long legs. "Would you like a new experience?"

"No," said Roger. "That is—"

"I mean, I could lend you a nightcap also. You would look charming in a nightcap." She and Cornelia laughed behind their fans.

"I shall not stay," burst out Roger. "I have already promised to come back in a week's time and bring two friends—as you asked me to," he said meaningly to Dulcibella.

"Well, if you won't stay tonight, you won't," said Dulcibella beginning to walk away. "I shall see you on Friday when I dine at the hotel. You can present the young men to me then."

She left them, with a last significant look at Roger.

8

Roger sat down again beside Cornelia; he would have liked to go, but he did not want to be the first, and obviously the recognised time for leaving had not yet come. It was seven o'clock; the unusual dining hour had upset all his notions.

"I'm puzzled," he said.

"Of course you are; it's the house," said Cornelia. "Don't let it worry you: it's not your affair. Tell me: who are these men you are bringing over?"

"Two of the party—the digging party."

"What are they like?"

Roger thought: what were they like?

"How old are they?" prompted Cornelia.

"The leader—Riley—is about thirty, I suppose. I don't know. The other one I shall bring is Martin Praa; he's a friend of mine."

Cornelia said suspiciously:

"Who asked you to bring them?"

"Your father did."

"Sure it wasn't Dulcibella?"

"Quite sure."

"But Dulcibella invited *you*!"

"I was the only one she had met."

Cornelia said in an urgent tone: "Did she mention *me*?"

"No—I don't think so," said Roger feebly: he hated telling verbal lies.

"Did she tell you anything about me?"

"I don't think so," he repeated.

"Did she tell you anything about—my father?"

"No. I gathered nothing about him except what we all know— that he will not allow us to look at the part of the mosaic that is on his land. We hope to persuade him otherwise, of course."

"You never will. Do you know about his obsession?"

"Joan Farmer, you mean."

"Do you know the effect it has—here?"

"I can see its effect on the house: you are living in the eighteenth or early nineteenth century as far as he can make you. I can see that the house is run on those lines candlelight, dinner at five and so on, no cars in the drive I wonder—"

"I'm not talking about the house!" said Cornelia furiously. "I'm talking about the effect on us—on *me*!"

"You mean"—Roger turned to look at her—"you are expected to live like a girl of that period?"

"A young lady, if you please. I am not allowed out unescorted. I must not correspond with anybody without my father's permission. I may not write a letter to a man, since I am not engaged to anyone, and young ladies don't write letters except to their affianced husbands."

"But why do you put up with it all? Why don't you clear out?"

"I will, some day—in my own time."

"Why not now?"

"I have no money: Augustus sees to that."

"But you could get a job."

"Perhaps I could. I don't know. I have never thought about it."

"Why not? It would be one way of escape for you."

"I don't want to work," said Cornelia, folding the fan and laying her hands in her lap.

"You don't?" This, to Roger, was inconceivable.

"No, I don't."

"Aren't you bored?"

"No," said Cornelia. "I am never bored, doing nothing. I am born to idleness. You would call me lazy, I suppose. *I* think you're all mad to work so hard."

"So you accept your father's ruling: you don't want to leave here."

"Oh yes, I do!" She sprang to life again, and two red spots appeared on her cheekbones. "I want it more than anything!"

"Then why don't you *do* something about it?"

"I shall."

Roger was baffled.

"You really mean to say, if you were asked to go anywhere—
dine out with a man for instance—your father wouldn't allow it?"

"He certainly would not."

"And you could submit to that?"

"I should think him justified according to his ideas. I think he
may be right from what I hear of the world nowadays, though
I don't know much nor wish to."

"But your stepmother—she dines at the hotel alone."

"Yes—once a week, on a Friday. She insisted on this before
she married him. He had to agree because he was madly in love
with her. Everybody is madly in love with Dulcie. Are you?" She
again raised her fan and gazed at him with her bright-blue eyes
over the top.

9

Roger said "No" automatically.

It was natural to him to say "no" because such an idea then
seemed to him absurd; but the truth was, it had not occurred to
him to ask himself the question, and even if the answer had been
"yes" he still would have said "no" to a stranger.

The question caused him considerable disturbance. He took
this to be annoyance at Cornelia's impertinent frankness. He was
annoyed with her just as he would have been if she had cheated
when playing a card game with him: people knew the rules, and
rules should be kept. But Cornelia had started in him a train of

thought which would continue long after he had left her. Roger would not have realised that he had fallen in love with Dulcibella if the question had not been put to him so brutally: it cut a way through all his preconceived notions, such as that one does not fall in love so suddenly, and certainly not with married women. Roger had not caught up with modern thought, and he considered love— falling in love at any rate—as a misfortune; to fall in love with a married woman was the sort of thing that did not happen to men like himself, or if it did it could easily be dealt with by repressive measures, change of air, injections of common sense. When he answered "no" to Cornelia's question, he thought the answer self-evident: but as he rode home on his Vespa that evening, he realised with a sinking of the spirits that this terrible thing had happened to him; moreover that it had been coming on for some time, ever since he saw Dulcibella in the hotel, sitting alone at her table, and wondered who she was; that it had been growing steadily worse, and Cornelia's probe had revealed it to him.

He was like a man who discovers that he has an incurable disease.

"What shall I *do*?" he asked himself; for Roger was a man of action. The sweet evening air seemed to fill his brain. "I shall have to take her from her husband: she is not in love with him—and he's old enough to be her father. Cornelia and she are like sisters." Cornelia had assured him of this.

How he was to do this he had so far no idea; but that it must be done he never doubted. He began to think of ways and means. But this was later. The conversation with Cornelia was not ended by his denial.

10

"No?" said Cornelia. "Are you sure? I hope you are sure, because my father would kill you, or cause you to be killed. He is a very ruthless man, and very observant, in spite of his appearance of being buried in the past."

"Tell me," said Roger, crossing his legs and watching Dulcibella as she moved among the guests, "does this obsession of your father's with the past really have much effect on *you?*"

Cornelia stirred. He knew without looking at her that the question raised in her both pain and anger, like the flick of a whip.

"Effect on *me?*" she said as if to gain time and wonder whether she should speak the truth or not. "It has *killed* me: can't you see?" She murmured to herself: "'Sweet, sweet, sweet poison.'"

"How can I see anything?" said Roger. "I didn't know you before." He stopped.

"Before what?"

He was confused, he did not know what to say.

"If you mean, since he remarried, I assure you Dulcie and I are the best of friends—like sisters."

"Yes," he said, "so I should have thought."

She gave him a look of mild scorn and went on:

"She is the only one who sees what has happened to *me*. She is the only one who has tried to help me. Oh," she interrupted before he could speak, "don't be deceived it suits her. We are partners of convenience only. I want to get out of here, she wants to get rid of me."

Roger was silent. He thought that she was being unfair but she spoke so vehemently, though quietly, that he was afraid to provoke her.

"Why did you quote Shakespeare just now? It *was* Shakespeare, wasn't it? *King John*. I remember doing it in school. 'Sweet, sweet, sweet poison for the age's tooth.'"

"Well, isn't it?" said Cornelia.

"Isn't what?"

"All this obsession with the past." There was a pause: at last he said:

"I still can't see why you don't clear out."

"I've told you: I don't wish to work. I am not qualified—I have not been brought up to work."

He would have liked to say, "Then you don't deserve any help," but again he dared not; besides he was not quite sure if this were true for her.

"My only escape," she said, reading his thoughts. "would be by marriage. But I meet no one here: my father sees to that."

"And why should he behave so irrationally? Even by his own standards—eighteenth-century standards, I gather —he shouldn't prevent you from marrying. In fact"—he laughed self-consciously—"he should surely arrange it."

"Oh," said Cornelia, "he will do *that*. *That* is one of the things I have to fear. He would *like* me to marry some rich man who would help him to maintain this place as a sort of museum—though not for visitors, of course. That professor you met at dinner will do very well: he is not rich, but he is a great scholar—among other things an expert on Regency furniture. They talk for hours—days— about furniture. My father wants to complete his collection. The Professor has the original table at which it is believed *that woman* wrote her infernal plays."

The venom in her tone was such that Roger could not believe that she was speaking of a woman who had been dead for nearly a century and a half.

"You mean Joan Farmer?"

"I hate her!" she said. "She has been the ruin of our lives. She ruined my mother's life. She will ruin Dulcie's —and her children's. It will all be repeated."

"Your brother: hasn't he got away?"

"Not he! He thinks he has: he goes in for everything that my father hates—sport, which apart from shooting my father doesn't recognise—and everything modern: music, dancing, flying."

"Good for him!" said Roger.

"Yes, but don't you see, Rupert is bored to death. He's rather a studious, artistic type. But he won't be governed by my father— and Joan Farmer. He's made a complete mess of everything so far, because it has been suggested by my father."

"What is he going to do?"

"I don't know. Go abroad, I suppose, and rot. He's living on my father at the moment. He hates Augustus. I hate Augustus. We both wish he'd die. It's the only thought we have in common."

Roger said nothing. He was shocked.

II

It was still light as he rode home.

When the lodge-keeper brought out the Vespa, he said:

"I hope you had a pleasant time, sir?"

"Very," said Roger conventionally.

"Funny people, eh?" The man grinned, watching Roger curiously.

Roger started the Vespa.

"The storm passed another way after all. But it'll come back. We have a lot of storms here: they do say it's the lie of the land."

Roger let in the clutch.

When he reached the hotel, he found Riley and the others in the bar.

"Now listen," he said to them, as they gathered round him, "I've got invitations for you, Riley, and one other —I thought Praa—for a week tonight, to stay for one night, possibly two. I'd better prepare you now while the impression of the place is on me. The house is a sort of enclave."

"What?"

"An enclave—a bit of the late eighteenth century enclosed and isolated in today. The owner—Augustus Gale has an obsession about Joan Farmer, the Regency playwright who was born there and died there. He won't let us dig up the mosaic on *his* side of the wall because over it is a mound where this woman had a summer-house or something, and used to sit and meditate and write."

"Did you," said Riley, "find out anything about the mosaic beyond the wall?"

"He has uncovered a bit on his side. I didn't see it: he'll show us the place when we go there next week. The rest is still buried under ten feet of sand and soil. The wall runs over it without interference, as you know. He intends to re-cover the part he has revealed."

"That's something, anyway," said Riley. "Then we can get him to let us look at the rest, provided we put the earth back afterwards. If we could get photographs—"

"Never!" said Roger. "He'll never let you move the earth. To him it's holy ground."

"Oh, rot!" said someone. There was a babel of angry protest from the group.

"He's quite serious," said Roger at last. "I don't think you'll change him. But you can try. I didn't say much, in case I queered the pitch for you." This was said to Riley. "You're more persuasive than I am."

They gave him a drink, and conversation became general. Roger smoked a number of cigarettes, but he did not enjoy them, or his company, as much as he had expected. He thought he would go for a walk, as it was still too early to go to bed. As he left he said to Riley: "I advise you to mug up the life and works of Joan Farmer."

"Why should I?"

"Because she's sitting on the mosaic, or her ghost is. Seriously, it's the only way to the old boy's heart."

Someone said: "How did you get on with his lovely wife?"

Roger said: "He has a lovely daughter, too." He gave Martin Praa a significant look.

III

Roger walked out of the hotel and took the path along the cliffs towards Geffrye House. He did this not because he was drawn towards the house but because there was no other walk except inland, and he wished to be near the sea. There was no danger of his reaching the house, it was too far, especially by the winding cliff-road: it could only just be seen during the day from where he was.

It was moonlight, and calm at present. The tide was in: he could hear it susurring against the base of the cliff. He could also see the storm-clouds piled on the horizon.

His mind was in a ferment: first, what could he do about Dulcibella? He never doubted that she would wish to leave Augustus and come with him: he identified her, at that moment, with Cornelia, who longed to escape and was only awaiting a rescuer. The chief trouble was that Roger's job was ill-paid, and Dulcibella was obviously used to every comfort—every eighteenth-century comfort, anyway—and even luxury. Roger certainly could not have afforded to buy her a dinner once a week in a hotel; he could not afford to dine, or stay, in hotels himself. The question was, would she want that sort of thing if she married him?

Already he was assuming that there would be a divorce and that they would be married as soon as possible. He firmly put aside, for the present, the thought of Augustus's character. But he could not keep out of his mind the recollection that Dulcibella had two children—two young children—by Augustus. He had seen them: they were real. He knew little about women, but he was sure from the books he had read and from what he had heard that they did not lightly abandon their children. If Dulcibella came with him she would want to bring the children. He would almost certainly have to keep them as well. He would not admire Dulcibella if she did not take this attitude. Of course, Augustus might refuse to let the children go: that would be the salvation of Roger, but it was not a solution he himself could put to Dulcibella, and anyway she might refuse to come unless the children came too.

Roger walked on as fast as he could: the cliff path was wide and grassy and not dangerous. The problem did not solve itself, though he dimly became aware that he would have to seek some different way of earning a living. He began thinking hard about this: the Colonies or Dominions perhaps? Someone called out:

"Hi, there! Wait for me."

He turned, to see in the bright moonlight the round face of Martin Praa.

"I followed you," said Martin simply: he was always simple in his approach, and this was sometimes deceptive. "I wanted to know what you were really up to."

"I don't understand," said Roger.

"Oh yes, you do! Come off it! Why *me*?"

"Why you—what?"

"Why have you chosen *me* as the second guest? You know I'm talking about what you're thinking about: this visit to—"

Roger capitulated.

"All right. I'll tell you." He reflected: he had no intention of telling Martin the truth. He said: "It's a queer set-up there."

"I know."

"But you don't know *how* queer."

"I'm listening."

2

Roger said: "The old man's mad."

"What old man?"

"Gale—Augustus Gale, the owner," said Roger impatiently. "You know he's trying to live in the eighteenth century."

"How so?"

"Every way: manner, dress, candles, everything. That mightn't matter, but it affects everyone around him. His wife, for instance, and his daughter." He could feel Martin eyeing him suspiciously. "His daughter's very attractive," he added boldly.

"I see," said Martin in his soft grumbling voice. "The wife for you, the daughter for me."

"You might do worse," said Roger. "And you haven't been all *that* successful, have you?" The odd thing was that Martin, though there was nothing wrong with him that his friends could see, had been singularly unlucky in love. He wanted to get married because he looked so young—almost babyish—and nobody took him seriously, or so he thought; yet he was ambitious. He knew he could not get the post he wanted unless he had a wife, that is, responsibilities. He also had thought that it would be pleasant to get away from his home, and his mother who adored him. He had been attracted to two or three girls and each had seemed to respond, and each had thrown him over at the last minute for someone else. Martin was puzzled and angry. The third girl, who had seemed a certainty, had been called Jessica.

"I thought of an answer to Jessica," he said triumphantly.

"I know you did," said Roger; Jessica was one of his cousins. "She told me."

"Did she mind?" said Martin eagerly.

"I don't think so," said Roger. "She laughed. It was a silly thing to do, you know—a damned silly thing." What Martin had done was to collect thirty new sixpences and send them by registered post to Jessica. "I don't think she got the idea at first. When she did, she laughed. Jessica is compounded of vanity: she was rather pleased that you bothered; she thought it showed how much you cared."

"It *was* a fag collecting the sixpences," said Martin ruefully. "I would have used threepenny-bits, but you hardly ever see silver ones nowadays."

"Silly ass."

"They were awkward to pack, too."

"You aren't supposed to send coins through the post."

"I know. You can if you like. I *did* like. Thirty pieces of silver!" He chuckled at his clever riposte to the faithless Jessica.

They turned back. The black cloud that had been on the horizon had quietly moved up the silvery sky and was threatening the moon. There was distant thunder, and forked lightning ran into the sea like quicksilver.

"So you think I should have a shot at this girl—what's her name?"

"Cornelia. You'd have to marry her."

"Of course."

"You're quite free. You want a wife. She wants a husband—at any rate she wants to get away from that old devil."

"You mean, she'll take anybody."

"Probably," said Roger incautiously.

Martin gave a throaty laugh.

"And you're after the wife?"

Roger said nothing. His feelings for Dulcibella were too new and real for him to bandy jokes about her yet.

"What's for poor old Riley?"

"The mosaic," said Roger, "if he can get it."

"He'll be useful, anyway," said Martin, "in distracting Gale's attention."

The first heavy drops of rain began to fall. They ran.

3

Dulcibella was at her usual table, alone, on the following Friday. Roger was at his place with the rest of the party. He could not wait, he could not control his nerves well enough to come in nonchalantly late as he had done before. He could no longer even look at her. He occupied himself with eating, and no one said anything to him: the matter, they were aware, was not a joke.

Roger had suggested to Martin and Riley that he should present them to her either during or after dinner. The three sat on after the others had left the table; and Roger, when he judged the moment suitable—when Dulcibella had reached the coffee and Benedictine—made a sign to them and rose. They crossed the room to the platform where she sat, and they felt foolish as even confident people do when they have to act under critical observation.

"Good evening," said Roger. "These are the guests you—Mr. Gale—have invited for—for tomorrow." He was not quite sure for how long they were invited. "This is Riley, the leader of our expedition. Riley, Mrs. Gale. And this is my friend Praa—Martin Praa, Mrs. Gale."

"Ah," said Dulcibella with understanding. "You will be most welcome. I hope your visit will not be unfruitful."

Roger looked at her, startled.

"I mean," she went on coolly, "I hope, Mr. Riley, you will succeed in persuading my husband to let you continue your work, if that's what you want."

"We do indeed, ma'am," said Riley. "We do indeed. We want to see the rest of that mosaic more than anything in the world." Riley had a slight brogue when he wished to be engaging.

"You are strange people, you archæologists," said Dulcibella, "and fortunate. Most men want much more difficult things."

"Then you're on our side?" said Riley, a little lost for all his knowingness.

Dulcibella took a cigarette and waved it about, waiting for a light. Roger got there first.

"I mustn't say that, must I" she said, inhaling deeply. "That might imply disloyalty. It's just that—I like people to get what they want."

"Do you?" said Roger in a low voice as he leaned towards her. "Do you?"

She stared at him for what seemed a long time— so long that he was afraid the others would notice. "If," she said slowly, "their wants don't clash with mine."

She turned to Riley: "I'll tell you plainly, I don't think you'll succeed. I don't think you can find any argument that will persuade my husband to let you move the earth of that mound. I suppose Roger has explained to you why?"

Roger's heart leapt at her sudden use of his name.

"I understand," said Riley, "that the place is sacred to him because of its associations with the playwright-woman."

Dulcibella stubbed out her cigarette: the action looked angry, but when she spoke her voice was calm.

"My husband, Mr. Riley, is in love with a ghost—or rather, with a woman who has been dead for nearly a century and a half; for I need hardly tell you, he has never seen or claimed to see her ghost. My husband is not mad." Martin and Roger exchanged glances. "He is simply suffering from the inexorable barrier of time, which is crueller than space." She stopped.

"Go on," said Roger softly.

"You will think me too metaphysical. I am not that. All I meant was that space can be traversed if one has a will. Time can *not*. *Any* barrier can be overleapt except the time-barrier. That's true, isn't it?"

They murmured agreement.

She rose and held out her hand to Riley. "We shall expect you tomorrow, then." She gave her hand to Martin. "For dinner? We dine, as I suppose Roger will have told you, at five."

She did not give her hand to Roger. He followed her to the door.

"How are you getting back?"

"I have a hired car."

"I wish I could take you."

She laughed. Her laugh was charming. "But you have only a Vespa."

"How do you know?"

"I saw you riding up to the gate last week, when you came to dine. You looked ridiculous—and perfectly sweet."

He blushed.

"Dulcie, let me drive back with you now."

"In a hired car? No, you would hate it. You see how well I know you, Roger. Besides, it would be too short— the drive, I mean."

"I want to talk to you."

"Yes, we have much to talk about. But you shall have your opportunity, when you come."

"How?"

"Leave it to me—I will arrange it."

They went through the swing door of the hotel, together yet absurdly separated. The evening was warm. She gathered a wrap about her shoulders, went without him down the steps and into the waiting car. The door was slammed by the porter. She waved to him. She blew him a kiss. She was gone.

Roger turned away, desolate. He did not believe in tomorrow, only in today—and today was over.

IV

When Roger got back he went straight to the bar. The other members of the party were all there. They looked at him seriously but said nothing—nothing, that is, about Mrs. Gale. They sensibly recognised that Roger was not in the mood to stand any jokes on this subject. Roger, when he lost his temper, was formidable.

After a suitable interval Riley came over to him and began discussing arrangements for the following day.

"You won't be able to take the car," said Roger.

"Why not?"

"Because Gale doesn't recognise the existence of cars. He won't allow them inside the gates."

"Then how do we get there?"

"I'll take Martin on the Vespa. You'd better get someone to drive you out and come back."

"We'll all go in the land-brake. Crowley can take it back. Now what is our plan of campaign?" Riley went on without waiting for an answer: "I'll tackle Gale about the mosaic. Have you any suggestions?"

Roger offered some suggestions, which were not listened to. They were merely concerned with tact and caution. Riley was persuasive, but his confidence in the inevitability of his success made him careless; and Augustus Gale was not a man who could be handled lightly. Roger tried to express this but was aware of making no impression on Riley's vanity.

"Leave it to me," was all Riley had to say at the end of a short period of not listening.

Roger sighed.

Riley slithered off the high stool; he and Roger never got on very well, because Riley mistook Roger's pessimistic attitude for mistrust, and this he could not bear.

"Bring your bag of tricks," he said casually. Roger's "bag of tricks" was his case of chemical reagents. "We may need it."

"I doubt it," said Roger.

"And bring your first-aid kit."

"Why?"

"Oh, I don't know. I always like to have it handy."

"All right," said Roger, even more gloomily. He knew well that Riley would like him to play the witch-doctor if the slightest occasion arose: cither by testing some specimen and pronouncing on its composition or date, or by performing some miracle of healing. Roger knew only a little about healing; but he was the only one of them who knew anything at all, so that it devolved on him to deal with cuts, burns and other results of minor accidents. He had once reduced a dislocated knee, almost by luck it seemed to him at the time; and he had once pulled out a tooth, an experience that still made him sweat to think of. He carried a number of instruments, bandages, and things in bottles. The bottles were all labelled; the contents were largely unused, and he wondered if they were still active enough to be any good. He liked attending to injuries better than his own job, and would probably have become a medical student if his parents could have afforded the fees, and could have kept him during the long years of his training.

2

The car, a land-brake used by the archæologists for carrying their equipment to and from the site, called at the hotel to take them to dinner. Warned by Roger, they left at twenty minutes past four, and alighted at the gate, grumbling at having to carry their small cases. Roger had three: one containing the necessaries for the night; one containing chemicals used on archæological tests, and one containing first-aid kit.

As they were standing in the hall, Dulcibella came out of the drawing-room and Cornelia came down the stairs. Both greeted them, though Cornelia had to come second.

"Robert is helping in the kitchen," Dulcibella said in an aside to Cornelia. "We shall have to show these gentlemen to their rooms—this way, Mr. Riley, please."

She led the way up the stairs, apologising for the lack of staff. Cornelia took charge of Roger and Martin. Having shown Martin to his room and left him, she signed to Roger to follow her.

"Why have you brought three cases?" she said. "The others have only one each. I hope it means that you are staying longer."

Roger explained.

"Oh!" she said archly. "I hoped you had brought changes of clothes—or at least pyjamas." She gave him a meaning look which he tried not to register. "Show me! I shan't believe you unless I see for myself. I'm a scientist, too, you see: I require first-hand evidence."

Roger, to avoid further badinage, opened the case of chemical reagents. He gave her some idea what each little bottle contained and what it was for.

"Oh, and are any of them poisonous?"

"Not these," he said, closing the case. "It was idiotic to bring it, because I shall have no occasion to use any of them *here*. But Riley asked me to."

"Do you always do what you're asked? I shouldn't have thought so: you look—stubborn."

"I don't think I am."

"I do. However, show me the other case."

He opened the first-aid case.

"Oh," she said, "but this isn't the ordinary kind. You've got instruments, and more things in bottles." Dulcibella entered and came up to them. "Look here, Dulcie! Look at these instruments of torture! What are they? Can you really use them?"

"That's a tooth-forceps," said Roger, taking it out and holding it towards the two women, who shrank back. "Once I did take a tooth out with it when a chap was in great pain and we couldn't get him to a dentist. It was in Crete," he murmured, recollecting. "I think I suffered more than he did."

"Did you have no anæsthetic with you?" said Dulcibella.

"Not then. I carry a syringe, and a local anæsthetic now, but I've never had occasion to use it, I'm glad to say."

"You sound sorry," said Cornelia.

"Perhaps I am."

"You are cruel."

"Far from it, I assure you."

"I didn't mean it as a criticism. I admire cruelty in the right place."

"In the right place? You mean, when good is achieved by causing pain."

"Yes."

"Then it wouldn't be cruelty," said Roger.

"It might be," said Cornelia.

"Don't be so metaphysical," said Dulcibella. "There isn't time. Dinner is served at five, as you know."

Cornelia paid no heed. "What's that?" she said, pointing to a bottle of pink tablets labelled poison.

"That?" Roger took it out and held it up. "Those are tablets of mercury biniodide. Now they *are* poisonous." He held the bottle out to Cornelia, who shrank back.

"Why do you carry them?" said Dulcibella.

"In case I should ever have to perform another minor operation such as lancing a boil or sewing up a cut. I've done that, too, in my time."

"But why should you want poison?"

"These tablets are dissolved in water, and the solution is used for sterilising instruments."

Dulcibella said: "Mr. Royden, will you come down when you're ready? I want you all to meet my husband, and perhaps see the children if it's not too late." She went.

"She's angry," said Cornelia. "I must go. Or rather, she's afraid of Augustus. You've no idea how Augustus dominates this place, and all of us—even Dulcie."

"I think I have," said Roger.

"Not you: for people like you, people like us don't exist."

"I certainly don't quite understand you."

Cornelia laughed: "Of course you don't. Don't try. If you understood us, you might become like us—and you are much nicer as you are. Regard us as a houseful of ghosts, like poor Joan Farmer. But remain flesh and blood yourself, please." With a smile over her shoulder she left him.

3

The scene in the drawing-room when Roger entered was much as it had been before. There were the drawn blinds, the lighted chandelier, the group round Augustus at the farther end of the room. The children were just leaving as Roger entered, and he was glad of this: they were pretty children, but he did not want to associate Dulcibella with children. All the other members of the family were there: old Mrs. Gale, Augustus's son Rupert, the Professor, and Miss Smith, the secretary, hovering in the background. Cornelia and Dulcibella were standing together, and Dulcie had evidently been presenting Riley and Martin to Augustus. Roger looked again. There *was* something different.

Yes, Augustus—it was Augustus. As Roger approached the circle he saw that this time Augustus was wearing what looked like fancy dress. He was dark and bewhiskered as before; but he had on knee-breeches and shoes with buckles, and a very high cravat, and a cut-away coat with tails. Roger drew nearer, and saw without surprise that the coat was frankly a dark blue, the breeches cream-coloured, and that there was also a sage-green waistcoat. This dress went well with that of the ladies, which was the same as before, or similar, and suited them well.

"Now," said Dulcibella, "here is Mr. Royden. You remember him."

"Ah yes," said Augustus with a slight bow. He did not offer his hand. He yawned, and used the hand to cover his mouth. "How do you do? My dear, I hope dinner will not be late."

"I don't think so," said Dulcibella. "It's still only two minutes to five. They are short-handed in the kitchen, but they are doing their best. Robert is helping."

"I am not interested in the kitchen," said Augustus with another yawn.

"Quite right," croaked old Mrs. Gale beside him. "It my young days—"

"Those were a long time ago," said Dulcibella tartly.

"Everything here is a hell of a long time ago," said Rupert suddenly. Roger looked from one to the other of the speakers—contestants, they might be called—in surprise.

"Rupert!" said Augustus in a thunderous voice. "Please to remember there are ladies present."

Rupert made a disrespectful sound and strolled away to the window. Luckily at that moment dinner was announced. Robert, the handy man, flung open the door so hastily that it crashed against a cabinet and made the contents rattle. Augustus marshalled his forces. He was in some difficulty: there were six men and only four women. He gave Dulcibella a lowering look as if to say, "This is badly arranged!", but she took no notice. She began enforcing her own arrangements.

"Augustus and Rupert, you will take the head and foot of the table. Professor, you will take in Mrs. Gale, and she will sit on my husband's left hand. Mr. Riley, will you take in Miss Smith and sit at my husband's right hand? I'm sorry that these arrangements are possibly not quite orthodox, but as you see we have six gentlemen and only four ladies, and Mr. Riley, I'm sure you and my husband have much to talk about." Augustus gave her a hard look, which she ignored, unless perhaps her dimpling smile had reference to him. "Mr. Praa, will you please take in Miss Gale, and seat yourself beside Miss Smith?" Martin looked round wildly for "Miss Gale" and was rescued by Cornelia who came smiling towards him and took his arm. They followed behind Riley with Miss Smith, and the Professor with Mrs. Gale, their pace slowed down to that of the elderly couple leading the way. Augustus and Rupert stood one on each side of the door, each glowering in his fashion. These arrangements left Roger and Dulcibella: she took his arm and guided him to the dining-room and to the right seat beside her at the bottom of the table.

4

"Are you content," she said as they walked across the hall, "with my dispensations?"

Roger, aware that Augustus and Rupert were close on their heels, nevertheless answered boldly:

"They are perfect!"

The meal proceeded without incident. Augustus looked dark and thunderous, and scarcely able to converse. The three guests were mostly silent; Roger wondered what his friends were making of this extraordinary set-up, and whether they felt as astonished as he had done a week before. So far as he could see Riley was at his ease, Martin most uncomfortable. The harsh voices of the Professor and Mrs. Gale senior were heard now and then, and once Cornelia laughed. But Roger, having been through this before, had adjusted himself to it all. In the yellow light the scene was as unreal—and as interesting—as a picture from the past. Only one thing was wrong. Apart from the dresses of the archaeological guests—for the Professor and even Rupert had conformed to some extent— there was only one servant, this Robert they all mentioned. He now reappeared in a white coat, but his face and hands were red, and he served clumsily. He also breathed heavily. At one moment it seemed as if Augustus were going to lose his temper, but Dulcibella intervened, sending Robert out of the room for something…

There was tension.

The tension was not relieved until the ladies rose. The Professor and Rupert went after them. The Professor said:

"You will excuse me, sir. You know I have now been forbidden any form of alcohol." Rupert, having held open the door for the others, followed them without apology. Augustus turned to Riley as soon as the door was closed, and said:

"The manners of the young have sadly deteriorated."

"Really?" said Riley politely. He was about thirty himself and was growing bald. "I think that in many ways they have improved: less formal courtesy, perhaps, and more real consideration."

Augustus, unused to being contradicted, said:

"Pass the port, gentlemen. Let us remain friends as long as we can."

"Sir," began Riley, thinking that this was a challenge.

"No, no," said Augustus, "not over the port. To your health!" He tasted the port, and to their dismay, threw the glass across the room. A red stain dripped down the wall. Augustus jumped up and pulled violently on the bell-rope. Robert appeared, no longer in his white coat, with his shirt sleeves rolled up. He had now become, evidently, a washer-up. He looked scared.

"You fool!" raved Augustus. "What filthy rubbish is this you have served to my guests? Are you incapable of distinguishing—?

Take this away, and bring me what I told you to bring." Robert removed the decanter and almost ran out of the room. He paused at the sight of the broken glass and the wine running down the wall, but scurried out at another violent gesture of Augustus's.

"The fool!" went on Augustus after the door closed. "I did not know I had such raw stuff in my cellar. And now—that—that— oafish creature will ruin—I think I'd better go—" He sprang up and went to the door, but returned before opening it. "Empty your glasses, gentlemen, into this bowl." He brought a glass fruit bowl from the sideboard. "You cannot drink this dreadful concoction. I must look to my cellar, I see."

They obeyed him. Roger had tasted the port, and could not tell that there was anything wrong with it, but dared not say so.

"The cook may put it into her plum puddings," said Augustus with a ghastly laugh. "I am afraid our evening is ruined. But we shall do better tomorrow. I think we had better join the ladies."

Roger felt Martin's elbow in his ribs as they followed Augustus and Riley across the hall to the drawing-room. They saw the wretched Robert approaching from the rear of the house. He was carrying a cobwebbed bottle by the neck with considerable carelessness, and they were glad Augustus did not turn and see him.

Robert, bottle in hand, stood still, staring after his master with dislike. As they passed him he made a disrespectful gesture with his thumb.

"Bats!" was all he said as he turned and walked back, now frankly swinging the bottle like a club.

Roger and Martin exchanged a look.

5

In the drawing-room all was peace, and boredom.

After the flutter of their arrival was over Augustus said to Dulcibella:

"I think, my dear, we will have tea first, and then I will take our guests to see the museum."

"Tea!" said Roger to himself. "What a horrible idea!" He had forgotten that this was the usual practice in the era in which Augustus was living.

"I assumed," said Dulcibella, in her sweet, smooth tones which sent a tremor through him, "that that was what you would wish. I have already rung for tea, and as no one appeared in answer to the bell, I have asked Cornelia to go and see—"

Augustus for a moment looked angry again. "Robert," he said, "was otherwise engaged." He seemed about to begin another tirade about Robert's crime when the door opened and a small procession entered headed by Cornelia. Behind her came Robert in a black alpaca coat and with his sleeves rolled down, carrying a huge tray and on it a tea service, everything very large: silver sugar bowl, and a set of very fine Wedgwood china. He placed the tray on a table which already stood before Dulcibella and began arranging the cups and saucers, and placing in each saucer a very large silver teaspoon. He was followed by an elderly maid carrying a very large silver teapot, and behind her came another with a silver tray bearing an urn under which was a methylated-spirit lamp.

Roger came out of his dark corner to help Dulcibella to hand round the cups. Martin and Riley followed their example. But Dulcibella had risen from her place.

"Cornelia, do me the favour of presiding. I'm tired." Cornelia took her seat and began pouring out the tea. She was helped by Roger, Martin and Riley, whom she had to instruct. Martin was asked to bring hot water from the urn, Riley was sent round with cups of tea, Roger followed with milk and sugar. When they all returned and stood in front of her awaiting fresh orders, she poured out tea for Martin and Riley, and was about to pour a third cup when Roger said:

"No tea for me, thank you." He had already taken the cup, absently, which she had gone on pouring out.

"Then give it to my father."

He did so. He looked round the room, wondering what to do next, when he saw Dulcibella smiling at him from the dark corner he had vacated. He joined her.

"This is fantastic!" he said, as she made room for him beside her. "How can you bear it?"

"I can't."

"But you must have known—"

"No. I knew him only as a clever, romantic man who needed companionship. I didn't know the extent of his obsession."

"Dulcie, let me release you!" He spoke very softly because old Mrs. Gale and the Professor were playing some card game—it looked like cribbage—nearby. Mrs. Gale made a noise as she drank tea through her teeth; Roger took advantage of these intervals. Dulcibella said:

"How can you release me, as you call it?"

"Come along with me."

"But—your career."

"I have no career. That's just it. I'm not rich. But I think I could make a new career if I had you. We could go abroad. Would he divorce you?"

"Promptly. He has nothing against divorce. I have often heard him say so. You see, his precious Joan Farmer married an actor who deserted her, and *she* couldn't get rid of *him*. A woman couldn't get a divorce for desertion until recently, as you know."

"Why should that matter—now?"

"It matters to Augustus. He longs to think of Joan Farmer as free."

"I see," said Roger slowly, in his 'lost' voice. Dulcibella smiled as she explained.

"He can't bear to think that she threw away the name under which she became famous—is famous all over the world—for a common name like that of her husband who was called something like Jones or Lewis."

"Owen," supplied Roger.

"You know?" For a moment he could have thought she looked displeased, or even frightened.

"I mugged it all up. *You* told me to," he said, and her smile returned.

"I was afraid," she said, "*you* were falling for her, too."

"For whom?"

She turned on him her large dark eyes, but did not answer.

"Then you will come! When can we go?" He incautiously laid a hand on hers and withdrew it, looking up hastily to find that there was no one between and him Augustus. But Augustus appeared not to have been looking in their direction.

"Are you sure?" she said in a low voice. "For you it is serious. For me it is less so. I have my children."

Roger's spirits sank.

"You'll bring them?"

"Of course. I shall leave here, not tomorrow, I couldn't be ready in time—but on Monday if you like. I shall leave quite openly."

"But your husband?"

"He won't be unduly surprised. He knows I care nothing for him."

"But won't he object to your taking the children? He can claim them legally, if you leave him."

"I know. That's why I shall bring them. I couldn't leave them here, in this atmosphere." It was her turn to lay a hand on his. "Don't be afraid, Roger dear: I'm not helpless. I can work. I have some money and some diamonds that are worth money. I will sell the diamonds and I will keep the children with my own money and my work till they grow up."

"It's not that."

"Oh yes, it might be! Men like making children, but till they are middle-aged they don't like having them around. You are so young"—she laughed—"one can see the egg on your beak."

"But—"

"Well?"

"Is it quite fair to *him* to take them as well as you? Won't he be quite shattered?"

"He will marry again and have another family. One of the reasons I want to leave him is that I am not willing to produce the number of children he thinks requisite, that is, by early nineteenth-century standards. Joan Farmer was one of thirteen children, and her brother and sisters each seem to have had ten at least." She smiled. "I have had two of his. I will have no more. I will have two of yours if you wish; but you'll have to keep *your* two."

Roger, shocked, delighted, thrilled all at once, did not know what to say.

"I," she went on coolly, "am completely of my time. I am bored with the past at its best; often I hate it. The future—does not exist, either. I have my own room; I mean, I don't sleep with Augustus. My room is near yours."

Roger said: "Not in this house."

Dulcibella stared at him, amazed. "How strange you are! What can it matter? Still, perhaps you're right Augustus might catch us and that would be very undignified. We will leave on Monday. Have you a car?"

"No," said Roger, "only my Vespa."

Dulcibella laughed.

"Much as I love you, dear Roger, I can't ride on the back of a Vespa. I will take a hired car as usual to the hotel, and we'll go in it to the railway station."

At that moment Roger saw Augustus look across at them over his teacup.

"Where will we go?" he stammered, confused.

"To London. Then we'll think."

Augustus put down his cup and came across to them Roger's heart missed a beat. But when Augustus reached them he gave a small bow to his wife, and turning to Roger, said:

"Are you ready to come and see my museum?"

"Of course," said Roger quietly.

6

Augustus led them down a flight of winding stone stairs. Then he opened a wooden door studded with nails.

"This door," he said, "is not correct. I bought it, but it's fifteenth-century, I'm afraid. I have not been able to get one of the right period yet."

They followed him into a stone room that might originally have been a cellar. It was now arranged as a small museum, with glass cases round the walls and two or three in the middle. Augustus switched on the lights.

"Electricity is legitimate here," he said with a smile. "This was not a museum originally."

In the dim yellow light the three archæologists looked round, making no comment. Riley threw back his head: the ceiling was painted pink with black spots. Augustus, noticing his interest, said:

"In those days ladies liked to wear spotted muslin. I have a piece here—an original piece, from a dress of eighteen hundred and five." He led them across to one of the cases and pointed out a square of pink muslin with black spots, mounted in a small wooden frame. "This is not a genuine Farmer relic," he said, "but a neighbour kindly gave me this specimen from a dress which belonged to his great-grandmother."

The archæologists made suitable noises.

Augustus led them from case to case. There were some devoted to jewels, others to sewing materials, others to specimens of Joan Farmer's handwriting, and one very sacred case entirely given up to a framed lock of her hair. It was black.

In the middle of the room was a desk at which it was said that several of the great works had been written. There were glass cases containing first editions of these works. There was a spinet. And, most striking of all, at the far end of the room, lit from beneath by three enclosed oil lamps, like footlights or, thought Roger, like sanctuary lamps, was a full-length portrait of Joan Farmer herself.

They stood before it, the three irreverent men, and the devotee Augustus with head bowed—Roger thought as Augustus passed the portrait he gave it a sort of genuflection—and said nothing.

The figure was standing, with hands clasped, facing the painter. She wore long flowing robes and some kind of red cloak or shawl. Her hair was long and unbound.

Roger studied her face: it wore an expression of infinite sadness. As the oil-lamps gave an occasional flicker the parted lips seemed to move. He began to understand Augustus's hopeless devotion.

At last they turned away. As they left the room and Augustus switched off the ceiling lights, Roger glanced back before the door closed. The sanctuary lamps burned on before the portrait; the face of the woman portrayed seemed to express grief at their going, at being left alone.

The door closed.

As they went up the spiral staircase Augustus, leading the way with Riley, said:

"So now I hope you see why nothing will induce me to let you disturb the ground for the sake of your mosaics."

There was a painful silence, broken only by the sound of their footsteps on the stone. Riley said gently:

"May we see the place?"

"Of course," said Augustus, "tomorrow morning after church."

"God!" said Martin, under his breath as he thought. Augustus turned and said over his shoulder:

"He will be there too."

7

When they returned to the drawing-room, Augustus, after a short pause, asked Cornelia to sing.

"No," said Cornelia, "no, Daddy, not tonight, please!"

Augustus waved a hand towards the spinet. Cornelia, as if hypnotised, took her place and began to tinkle away and then to sing in faltering tones an old-fashioned song.

Roger seethed with indignation: the man was insufferable, ordering a grown-up daughter about in such a way, before strangers! He couldn't think why Cornelia obeyed. He half-formed the thought of crossing over to the spinet to take his place behind her and lend her support, when he saw Martin get up, lumber over in his elephantine way, and bend down low over her shoulder in an effort to see the right place at which to turn over the pages.

The scene was pretty, and from outside must have looked harmonious—a family party, though not of this epoch. But no one could look in from outside: the curtains were drawn.

Roger sat down on the sofa in the dark corner; Dulcibella had left, so there was no indiscretion. Near him old Mrs. Gale and the Professor had finished their game and were listening to and looking at Cornelia. When the song was finished, there was clapping—the thin clapping of a private party. Cornelia glanced at Augustus and by a wave of his hand he ordered her to continue. She stood up to look for music on the top of the spinet and Martin pretended to help her. Roger became aware of the elderly cracked voices beside him.

"She is a dear girl!" said old Mrs. Gale. "Professor, you are to be fortunate: more fortunate in your second marriage than in your first."

The Professor, stroking his small white beard, said:

"Madam, we must not speak ill of the dead, Solon says. But I must confess, I have hopes of greater happiness with this dear girl than with poor Helvig."

"She was a German, wasn't she? It's a mistake to marry a man or woman of a different race."

"She was German. But I like Germans. I like their high seriousness, and I like the way they bring up their women—to be industrious, unexacting, *obedient*. Above all I value obedience. I am glad to see it has been instilled into your granddaughter."

"Oh," croaked old Mrs. Gale, "Cornelia can be wilful enough when she chooses! But her father can control her. *I* taught him to obey *me* when he was little: I had to be father and mother to him as I had no husband— my husband left me when Augustus was only four." Her voice became harsher, with anger at this event of half a century ago. "He is self-willed now, but I never allowed him to be so with *me*. I beat him. He is a fine man."

"Yes, a fine man," echoed the Professor. "But he has his weaknesses."

"What do you mean?"

"Surely you see what I see."

"Tell me what you mean."

The Professor leaned back. "His second marriage is not as happy as I expect mine to be."

"Speak out!" hissed the old lady.

"His charming second wife is not suited to him. She is too young, too beautiful to be confined here. She is a ripe plum: she will fall at a touch. I think she is flirting— I don't say it's more, I couldn't hear what they were saying—with the young archæologist."

"Nonsense! She wouldn't dare!"

"Mrs. *Augustus* Gale, dear lady, would dare anything."

"You're right," said old Mrs. Gale. "I must warn my son."

"Don't be hasty," lisped the Professor. "You have nothing to report—yet."

"But you said you *saw* something."

"I saw their heads close together. I cannot vouch for its being more than harmless whispering about something quite innocent. But their hands touched. It may have been accidental, but I doubt it."

"I opposed the marriage," said old Mrs. Gale. "I told him he was making a fool of himself to remarry when he had a grown-up daughter. And his wife—Dulcibella—is most unsuited to him, I agree—to this house." She leaned confidentially towards the Professor, and Roger had to strain his ears: his hearing, however, was acute, and even her lowest voice was penetrating. "I will say—I don't approve of Dulcibella, or like her, as you know, but I do think Augustus goes much too far."

"With his cult of the past, you mean?"

"Yes. It gets worse. It started as a hobby, but now even I am bound to say it's an obsession. It's taking new forms, and it's getting really rather trying. The servants, for instance; we only have Robert and the cook, and a daily woman from the village: nobody else will come. But Augustus expects us to live as if we had an indefinite number of servants, including a butler and a housekeeper. It falls rather heavily on the women of the household —especially as Dulcibella takes no notice. It falls on Cornelia and me to keep things going."

"I understand," said the Professor. "Yes, I think he carries the Joan Farmer cult too far. Why don't you speak to him?"

"Even I wouldn't dare!" said old Mrs. Gale.

"Oughtn't he to see a doctor? A psychiatrist?"

She threw up her small yellowish hands in a gesture of despair.

"Impossible! And, anyhow, there's no need. Sometimes I wonder how it will end. I wish you would speak to him."

"Not I," said the Professor. "If anyone does so, it must be you—his mother."

"If my observation corroborates yours, I shall have to. Meanwhile, Professor, don't encourage him any more in this cult, will you?"

"I?" He began to protest. But he had to break off, because Cornelia's performance on the spinet had finished; they had talked all through it. She closed the instrument and, leaving Martin in the lurch, came over to sit beside Roger.

"Capital, my dear!" said the Professor, leaning over to take her hand. She snatched her hand away as if his touch were that of a hot iron.

"Did *you* like it?" she said to Roger.

"No," said Roger shortly. "I hated the whole thing. Oh," as she withdrew, "not your singing and playing—the whole performance. It disgusted me."

He got up and left her and went to sit with his two friends at the other end of the room.

8

The night passed without incident. Roger, lying awake, heard doors opening and shutting, and an owl hoot. He was haunted, even more than by Dulcibella's living charms, by the sad face of Joan Farmer looking out from her picture.

The morning was bright, with blue sky and big white clouds. Roger walked to the little church with the family. He was the only one of the archæologists who could attend the service of the Established Church: he was an Anglican who, having been confirmed at the age of eleven, had rapidly lost interest and ceased to attend. Riley was a Catholic: a lapsed Catholic, but still tied to that faith. Martin was a sturdy Dissenter, a Wesleyan Methodist.

As Roger knelt by himself in the pew behind the family in the attitude of preliminary prayer, he looked round the grey walls and enjoyed the familiar smell of damp that recalled his childhood. He took in the gayer Sunday clothes of the congregation, including his own party, and thought how odd it was that the woman who knelt in front of him—and Dulcibella really knelt, she did not "squat" —the woman in the little straw hat and the blue dress, should be his, not really the wife of the forbidding-looking man beside her.

As he watched the nape of Augustus's neck, overgrown with long black hair, Augustus sat back so suddenly that he took Roger by surprise and almost collided with him. Roger sat back too. He noticed Augustus give an upward glance to the left before he opened his prayer book. On the wall were a few memorial tablets to earlier parishioners; they were of the usual kind, white marble with urns and weeping willows and extravagant praise of the dead. Then, Roger was startled to see on the wall, just above Augustus's pew, a large bronze tablet, obviously recent, with only one name on it in large Roman script, very different from the cramped black script on the marble tablets. The name was:

JOAN FARMER

He looked again, and read:

In this Church
lie buried the earthly remains of

JOAN FARMER

A great woman
Now universally recognised and beloved.

In her short lifetime
She worshipped here.

This tablet to her immortal memory was erected
by Augustus Gale in the year of Our Lord,

MDCCCCXLVIII.

The whole was surmounted by an open book, and enclosed by a border of what looked like laurel-leaves. Now Roger understood Augustus's glance, and the triumphant smile which, he could just see, accompanied it. Augustus was in communion with the dead; he was telling her:

"I am here, as usual. I have come to pay homage. I have mentioned you in my prayer."

9

After the service Roger walked out of the church with the Gale family and waited while they talked to acquaintances outside. At the gate of the churchyard they were met by Riley and Martin, and Augustus detached himself from his family and came with them.

"Perhaps," said Riley, "you'd like to see what we've done on our side of the wall, first."

Augustus gave an ungracious grunt of acquiescence.

They took a path, damp and slippery with moss, outside the walls of Geffrye House, and reached the excavations after a walk of about a quarter of a mile. Riley took charge and began explaining the work. It was extensive and deep, and a pebbled ramp led down to the level of the mosaic. Two or three of the party were there, presiding over the activities of half a dozen workmen, who were sitting on the ground cleaning the uncovered mosaic, smoking and talking. What was not being cleaned was covered with tarpaulins.

"It is essential," said Riley in his most professional manner, "to protect what we have uncovered. You can see that a heavy downpour of rain or a ground frost at night, such as are all too common even at this time of the year, might dislodge large numbers of the *tesserae*, destroying the picture and making it impossible for us to restore it."

"What are the workmen doing?" said Augustus.

"They are replacing loose *tesserae*. And in the places where you see there has been subsidence, they are going to remove squares of the *tesserae* en bloc, fill up the ground to the proper level, and restore the mosaic. You see," he pointed, "where our trained men have a square laid face downwards and are applying a further coat of white cement which will hold the existing *tesserae* together and enable us to fit in any loose ones. When it is turned over it will look exactly as it did in the Roman owner's day."

"And what does it represent?" said Augustus, casting a contemptuous look over the whole extent of the pavement, which was a very fine one.

"It's a hunting scene," said Riley. "You see here where it's completed a fine representation of a wild boar pursued by dogs and spearmen. That's the east walk. On the west here you have the bathing establishment of the villa—the excavations of this part, and of the *triclinium* or dining-room, are not yet completed. They run from east to west, under your wall." He gave a significant look at the high rough wall that cut off the view to the west, and a glance at Augustus. But Augustus remained impassive.

"This corridor," went on Riley, "so far as we have excavated it, shows scenes suitable—considered by the Romans suitable—to a dining-room and to their baths. The *triclinium* shows the edge of a drinking scene. The *sudarium* shows—" He waved a hand and they bent their gaze to the floor where several large Roman girls sported naked, or nearly so, with balls and other implements of their sports such as the discus.

"Aren't they magnificent?" said Riley, winking at Roger behind Augustus's back.

"Disgusting!" said Augustus venomously. "What barbarians!"

"Oh, but, sir—"

"If they hadn't been done by Romans some two thousand years ago—"

"Fifteen hundred," corrected Riley automatically. "We date this part of the villa as being fifth century A.D., when the Romans were soon to leave Britain. That's what makes it so remarkable: it must have belonged—been built by—a very rich, luxury-loving man, perhaps a wealthy Romanised Briton, an official. It's fit for an emperor. But rich Romans didn't stay in Britain if they could help it. The climate was too bad. So we think—"

"Cover it up," said Augustus turning away. "It's pagan art at its worst: nothing but sensuality, eating, drinking, women, sport.

We have enough barbarism of our own without your digging up ancient examples. Why can't you look back to the *civilised* past?"

He turned towards the wall, and Roger noticed the dedicated look which he had exhibited before the Joan Farmer portrait in the museum.

Riley said softly, with a touch of Irish in his tone:

"Then you are irrevocably set against our enterprise?"

Augustus didn't deign to answer.

"And you will not give us permission to continue our work under your wall?"

"Certainly not," said Augustus.

"Not though we promise you that we will restore everything— mound and wall—exactly as it was before? This is a big concession, but we could restore, photograph and perhaps protect the mosaic which, unfortunately, lies inside your boundary."

Augustus rounded on him.

"Twentieth-century barbarism! You think you could restore everything as it was by just putting back the earth you had disturbed! All you think of is material values! Have you never heard of desecration? How could you ever restore a place where your big boots and those of your colleagues and your workmen had trampled?" He had by now worked himself up into a rage and the vein down the middle of his forehead swelled. "Never, never! You shall never disturb a square inch of soil on the other side of that wall!"

"Then," said Riley, still softly, "we shall have to take other steps. I don't want to, but it will be my duty—my painful duty."

"Over my dead body!" said Augustus, and for once the cliché did not sound exaggerated as he threw out his long black arms, and his long black hair was lifted by the breeze.

"That's your last word?" said Martin Praa, as Riley stepped back.

"It is. But I bear you no ill-will. It's just that you're ignorant. You have the wrong standards, like most young men nowadays. It's the disease of the age: my own son is no better. Come back to the house and forget this— this nonsense." He gave a last contemptuous look at the Roman pavement, and walked away.

Riley called after him:

"Do you mind if we go round and look at what you have uncovered?"

Augustus jerked round.

"Follow me. I will show you. Excuse me, but I cannot trust you. It is not, as I have said, your fault. You are— merely uncultivated."

The three archæologists followed him.

I O

He led them back along the path outside the wall to a postern door, which he opened with a key. When they had passed through, he followed, shut the postern, locked it and turned to them.

"Follow the wall," he said, "to the right. I will leave you here and return to the house."

"Won't you come with us?" said Riley, trying to be propitiatory.

"No," said Augustus sharply. "I do not wish to hear your comments. You are my guests; I do not wish to be discourteous towards you. Please come back to the house when you have seen all you wish, and partake of refreshments. Stay as long as you wish, but I need not say, do not touch anything. And do not tell me of your opinion afterwards. The subject is now closed."

He turned and left them.

They looked at his retreating figure, black and stooping, as he skirted the wall.

"I suppose," said Riley, "we might do better to give up and go. I begin to be afraid we may exasperate him into doing something desperate."

"You can't go," said Martin eagerly. "We can't give up. The old boy is certainly nuts—but we can at least report on the site, say he's nuts and try to get him out of here."

"What do *you* think, Royden?" said Riley.

Roger tried to think impersonally. He was feeling, by now, badly about the whole thing. His desire for Dulcibella, his wish to get her out of this, almost overpowered his reason; but he could not help regretting that it involved him in disloyalty, treacherous disloyalty, towards his colleagues. He spoke out:

"I think we should stay."

"Till tomorrow."

"Till tomorrow. What time is the car calling for us?"

"I said ten," said Riley, "in case they had a late breakfast. I wish I'd said eight. I'll be thankful to get out of this." He turned to the right. "Let's go and look at the mosaic and see what kind of a mess he's been making. As you say, Praa, I can draw up a report."

They tramped off, in the opposite direction to Augustus, on the inside of the wall. In a few minutes they reached the part of the mosaic he had uncovered.

The mess was worse than they had expected. A pit had been dug revealing a few square yards of the mosaic, and left unprotected. There had been considerable rain. The sides of the pit sloped inwards towards the bottom, so that the opening at the top was much bigger than the area of mosaic revealed, which was not more than six square feet.

Riley climbed down carefully and began examining the sides and the floor. He signalled to Roger.

"Come down, will you? Be careful, though, it's slippery."

Roger jumped. He had noticed a trickle of earth when Riley climbed down and he wanted to avoid further damage to the sides.

The floor was covered with a sticky deposit of mud and sand. It was not level, so that there was a viscous puddle in the centre.

"God!" said Roger.

"Quite," said Riley. "It's a mess—already. The man's a criminal lunatic. But look here: let's keep calm and maybe we can *do* something. I want you to have a look at the sides."

Roger began his examination from the floor upwards. The first few feet of the cutting consisted of compressed sand with an admixture of earth. He took a specimen, put it in a box and labelled it. He always carried about with him numbers of small tin boxes, usually empty typewriter-ribbon boxes.

"Sand," he said, "with admixture."

"I thought so," said Riley. "How high does it reach?"

"I haven't got my foot-rule."

"Praa!" called Riley to Martin, who was longing to come down and join them in the confined square below. Martin jumped. For a heavy man he jumped well and alighted neatly, but the slippery floor was too much for his skill and he sat down on the mud. He was up again instantly.

"Got your foot-rule?" said Riley. He might as well have asked him if he had hands. Martin never moved without his measuring-kit except when bathing.

"Of course."

"Measure where Royden shows you and make notes. It's important for my beastly report."

Roger pointed out the sandy stratum. Martin measured with a metal rule which emerged, when pulled, from a round case, like a snake.

"Height from mosaic floor, four feet." He made a note.

"Look at the next stratum," said Roger, pointing and breaking off a piece of jutting substance like soft slate. He turned to Riley. "This is compressed alluvial deposit on top of the sand. The sand, the first deposit, was probably carried by wind—a storm."

"That's what tradition says!" Riley was excited.

"I know. This blew in and covered the mosaic: it's exactly as on our side, only here the sand is thicker. I've analysed it, as you know; it comes from the sand-dunes, or rather, I should say, it was brought here by the same gale that formed the sand-hills. Then comes a long period of settling of various earths on top; then more earth, and pressure. You can see the whole history."

"Do we have any idea about dates?" said Riley.

"No. Guesswork. But we can reckon on the sudden storm which brought the sand, some time before the villa was deserted—some time before the fifth century, therefore. Then centuries of slow silting and rain. Then, on top, the soft earth and the grass as usual. Then come these people—farmers—in the sixteenth century, I gather. Then they were bought out in the eighteenth century by a family called—curiously enough—Farmer. They built the wall, in glorious ignorance, right over the villa, and enlarged the house, or pulled it down and rebuilt it. Then you reach the early nineteenth, and this woman who fascinates Gale."

"Yes. That's history. Praa, make me diagrams—plans, sections. Make them look impressive. I shall want them if I appeal to the

Ministry of Works. If they declare this an Ancient Monument Gale will *have* to give way. If they don't, there's always public opinion."

Riley knelt down on the muddy floor and scraped away some soft mud. "Look at that! It's one of the Muses. Look, Praa! It's—" He scraped away more mud, revealing some Greek lettering in black on white. "It's quite clear, though some of the *tesserae* are missing, or loose. K—" Martin knelt beside him on the mud, and his fair hair fell over his brow as he peered. "K," repeated Riley. "What's this second letter, a V upside down?"

"Lambda," said Martin. "K-L-I-O. Clio—it's Clio, the Muse of History. Isn't that right?" He spoke over his shoulder to Roger. Roger said "Yes", and went on examining the sides of the pit and taking specimens. He had now got possession of Martin's foot-rule and was measuring.

"Then," said Riley, standing up and ineffectively brushing his muddy knees, "this is the end of the Corridor of the Muses. We began over there"—he pointed towards the wall—"with Thaleia and Melpomene—Comedy and Tragedy. We have the beginnings of the next one, and some letters that look like the end of the name... MNIA. You say Polyhymnia. Now can you figure out where this one would come in the line? They run under the wall and as there are nine—"

Martin reflected, got out another foot-rule from a pocket and measured Clio across her widest span, which was across the shoulders. He stood astride her.

"Let me see," he calculated, "this one must be the end, if the space is all filled up. She seems to be looking inward, towards another Muse."

"Yes," agreed Roger, "they're probably in pairs like the first two. Pairs with a space of at least three feet between each pair."

"And one odd girl out," said Riley. "They are nine."

"One in the centre," suggested Martin, "and two pairs on each side."

"Unless Mum is there too," said Roger.

"Which was Mum?" said Riley.

Martin supplied:

"Mnemosyne, Goddess of Memory."

"Oh yes, of course," said Riley. "Then we can surmise this corridor to be about—what would you say, Praa?"

"They're big women," said Martin, rubbing his chin. "I'd give each pair at least eight feet across, allowing for a space of a couple of feet between. One in the middle— say about four feet, with two feet each side. Four pairs with three feet between each pair and a blank space at *this* end as at our end; that gives a total length of, say, forty-eight feet. Of course, that's only an approximation—" He burbled on, covering himself up against possible conviction of error, and casting anxious glances at the high wall: "We could pace it out, from our side to the wall. And then from the base of the wall to here. Would you like me to climb over?" He looked eagerly at Riley as if longing to hurl himself at the high wall and escape from this prison.

"No," said Riley. "Let's get back now and 'partake of refreshments', as Gale says."

"Rather!" said Martin. "I'm starving. I suppose we shan't get a midday meal, even on Sunday? I suppose we have to wait till five?" He looked at Roger appealingly, as if Roger had something to do with these fantastic arrangements.

They climbed out of the pit, bringing down a little more earth in their scramble, and set out across a paddock to the house. When they were halfway across, Roger stopped.

"I say!"

"Well?" said Riley.

"Look here, you haven't looked at that mound."

"What mound?"

"That hillock where there used to be a summer-house."

"What summer-house?"

"Where Joan Farmer wrote some of her plays."

"Oh, damn Joan Farmer!" said Riley. They trudged on. They were hurrying, tired, dirty and inclined to be quarrelsome.

"I heartily agree," said Roger, bringing up the rear. "But remember, it's no use taking that line if you want to get round the old man."

"I wish he'd fall into that pit," said Riley savagely, "and break his blasted neck. Failing that, I wish someone would shoot him."

I I

As they approached the house, Riley, walking beside Roger, said:

"I say, do you think we could switch the old boy's passion to Clio, Muse of History? After all, what does it matter? One woman's dead, and one never existed, so as he can't have either, he might as well love Clio, and give us permission to excavate."

Roger didn't answer.

When they reached the porch steps the two children came flying out. They were wearing their Sunday clothes, and they looked rather absurd, especially the boy. None of these archæologists could have described what the children were wearing except that it had a good deal of lace about it.

"Hullo!" said the boy, whose name was Henry. "Where've you been? You're all over mud."

The little girl, whose name was Isabella, came up to them more quietly, and standing in front of Roger, said:

"You should not garden on Sundays."

"Why not?" said Roger.

"Papa says so."

"Oh, really! And what does Mummy say?"

"Who?" She looked puzzled. "Oh, you mean my mother. She doesn't say much, and it wouldn't matter if she did. She doesn't count, you know."

She stood in front of him and made this astonishing remark as if she were reciting a piece of poetry, with her hands behind her back.

"Oh, really?" said Roger. "Who says so?"

"Nobody says so. But Papa gives all the orders, except to the cook. And *he* says that Mama's place is to be obedient and do as she's bid."

Roger stared at the child in dislike. It began to dawn on him that he was going to have an excuse for leaving her behind.

"And what does your mother say to that?"

"She says nothing. I told you."

Henry was turning cartwheels on the circle of lawn. An awful voice boomed forth.

"Henry! Isabella!"

Isabella coolly dropped Roger a curtsy and went up to the steps. Augustus emerged into the porch, and stood at the top. Isabella dropped him a more formal curtsy and passed indoors. As Henry tried to run by, Augustus stopped him and boxed his ears. Henry howled.

Dulcibella appeared in the doorway.

"Augustus," she said quietly, "you are not to strike my children. I won't have it."

Augustus turned to her with a smile, and Henry bolted past them both indoors.

"*Your* children? They are mine, too, I presume. At least, madam, I have reason to hope so. I trust I am not mistaken."

"Augustus, you are going too far, as you will soon discover."

"Do you mean you intend to leave me? With which of these young men do you propose to elope? Beware, my dear madam. I am not as blind as you imagine, and there are others who serve as my eyes, and they are not blind either."

"You mean your mother?"

"I mean Mrs. Gale."

"I am Mrs. Gale, unfortunately."

"You are—fortunately or unfortunately—Mrs. *Augustus* Gale. If you disgrace me you will never see your children again; remember *that*, madam, if you are dead to all sense of shame."

The three archæologists standing below on the terrace were looking on and listening, appalled. They could not tell whether Augustus and Dulcibella knew they were being watched or not. They dared not even move away, in case they had not been seen and their movement would betray them.

Dulcibella said coldly:

"Augustus, you are mad. Why should I be loyal to you? You have never been faithful to me."

"What do you mean?"

"You are, and always have been, in love with a dead woman. I am entitled to a lover if I choose. You are the lover of—" She stopped.

Augustus stepped up to her.

She finished:

"A dead woman. Joan Farmer."

He struck her, not very hard, a light tap on the cheek. But on her delicate skin the mark of his three fingers was visible. Roger sprang at him.

The other two grasped him by the wrists and held him back. None of them said a word. Augustus took his wife by the arm and steered her towards the door. He said, without looking round:

"My dear, I think we should go in. I have seen our guests approaching. They will be in need of refreshment after all their explorations."

Dulcibella walked in without speaking. Augustus bowed and followed. The three archæologists stared at each other.

"Hadn't we better clear out?" said Martin.

"Certainly not," said Riley. "What do their family quarrels matter to us? We must keep our objective in mind. Let's go in and pretend we saw nothing. Roger, don't let your feelings run away with you, will you?"

"I'll try not to," muttered Roger.

"You're too chivalrous. Remember, our business here is solely with the preservation of the mosaic: the whole mosaic. It's what we're paid for."

"All right," said Roger sullenly. His mind was in a turmoil.

12

When they entered the drawing-room they found the family assembled, including the Professor. On tables were large silver trays, one bearing glasses of wine, another small sandwiches, another some kind of sweet cake. The three men looked at these with dislike.

"Come in, gentlemen," said Augustus. There was nothing in his manner to show that anything untoward had happened; in fact he spoke more cheerfully and hospitably than usual. "Come and take a glass of wine with me. You look tired."

Roger cast a questioning glance at Dulcibella. There was no longer any mark on her check, but her eyes had a smouldering look. He went boldly up to her.

"Is it all right about tomorrow?"

"Yes. I shall leave. You see now why I must bring the children."

"Of course," said Roger.

"I can't leave them here with him."

"What about your stepdaughter? Couldn't she look after them?"

Dulcibella laughed.

"My dear, Cornelia doesn't like them. One can hardly blame her: they are at present very ill-trained—spoilt one minute, too harshly treated the next, and *never* reasoned with. I could correct all that, but my authority over them is undermined."

"So I gather."

"But don't worry, poor dear. If you don't want us, we can always go elsewhere."

He tried to interrupt her, but she stopped him.

"I will call at the hotel tomorrow and see you. Probably we shall spend the night there. I shall know at once how you feel. You need have no fear: my release doesn't depend on *you*."

Cornelia approached them, and they were obliged to separate.

"My father asks you to drink wine with him. May I give you a glass?"

Roger took a glass. The wine was Madeira, which he disliked, especially before a meal. Then he remembered that there would be no meal till five. He heard Augustus say:

"Robert, fetch a glass of porter and a beef sandwich— with mustard, you said, sir?—for Mr. Riley."

Roger, as he sipped the sweet wine and walked towards Augustus, wished he had waited.

13

As Roger neared Augustus, Martin intercepted him.

"I say, look here!" He led Roger over to a table on which there were knick-knacks. "Do you see what I see?"

Roger looked. On a wooden board he saw a number of small cubes, black, white and a rusty red. He picked up a white one.

"Looks like sugar."

"Marble," said Martin.

"No!"

"Yes: about a cubic centimetre—the sides are not quite uniform. But there's no doubt what they are. Look here."

He picked up one of the red cubes: through the centre a hole had been drilled.

"My God!" said Roger. "*Tesserae!*"

Augustus was standing behind them.

"You observe I have discovered a use for the mosaic. I am going to make a necklace of it for my daughter. My daughter Cornelia will be satisfied with one long string. She is, of course, impressed by the rarity and originality of the gift, which will be hers when she marries. My daughter Isabella wants several strings and bracelets and anklets, too, so I shall have to get some more *tesserae* from the pit."

Roger said explosively: "You can't—"

Augustus looked at him with a smile. "It seems to me an excellent use for all these bits of stone, to make ornaments to bedeck young females. I understand from Professor Bose, who is my elder daughter's affianced husband" —he looked at Roger as he spoke, not at Martin—"that the picture formed by these little cubes is a crude representation of one of the Muses, Clio to be precise, the Muse of History. Did your investigation confirm this? Not that it needs confirmation, even by the learned. I myself have enough Greek left from my schooldays to discern the lettering—"

"You don't mean," said Martin, "you're going to break up the mosaic to make ornaments?"

"I regret," said Augustus, "to see that you disapprove of my plan. It seems to me a charming one. And since the Muse has been buried for at least fifteen hundred years, unseen by anyone, I hardly think she could object to giving a little harmless pleasure now."

Martin's voice rose to a squeak, as it always did when he was shocked, astonished or angry.

"But we thought you were going to cover it up—at least to leave it as it was, even if you won't let us do a systematic excavation."

"You thought wrong. I did not wish to hurt your archaeological feelings. But I must insist on the right to do as I please with *my own*."

Roger, fuming, but realising that anything he might say would make matters worse, wondered whether he had imagined the emphasis on the last two words. Did "my own" include not only Augustus's wife but his daughter? He resolved to have another talk with Cornelia, if he could get near her.

14

As he crossed the room he encountered Riley.

"Go over to that table," he said, "and look at what is on it. But keep quiet. We've got to stop the old devil somehow." He went on his way towards the table where Cornelia had now handed out the last glass of Madeira. He drew her aside.

"Are you really a party to that piece of vandalism?"

"What? I beg your pardon. Oh, you mean the mosaic."

"I mean the *tesserae* which your father is planning to make into necklaces and bracelets for you and your sister."

"Don't call that little beast my sister."

"She's your half-sister."

"You don't suppose these relationships mean anything to me? I judge people as they are, not as they are related to me by blood."

"You are more rational than most of us," said Roger.

She snapped back, as if this were an accusation: "I am not. I can love, Mr. Archæologist, as well as you, or better. I have a brother. I love him dearly."

"I'm sure you do," said Roger soothingly. He did not want to provoke the wrath that he saw gathering in those bright-blue eyes. "By the way, where is he? I don't see him here."

"He has gone out shooting. Papa expects him to do this in his spare time. Rupert loathes it. He never shoots anything—except fellow guests. He once shot Augustus in the leg—by accident, of course. But Augustus has more sense than to go out with him any more, so we shan't get rid of him *that* way."

Roger felt uncomfortable: he changed the subject.

"Is it true you are engaged to marry the Professor? Or in this house should I say 'betrothed' or 'affianced' or something?"

"No. Why?"

"Your father said so."

"In his mind," said Cornelia, "it is so. It is what he has decided for me. And the old man thinks it's all settled. But I shall have something to say about that, you know."

"I hope so," said Roger. "You're too young and beautiful to marry that old fossil."

"You think so?"

Roger was a little disturbed by her movement towards him, and the intense look in her almost too bright eyes. He thought: "I must ginger up Martin." Luckily at that moment there was a diversion. Rupert Gale walked in.

15

He had not bothered to change. He wore an old tweed jacket, and his boots were muddy and his short gaiters were wet. His father looked at him with annoyance and contempt.

"Kill anything?"

"No."

Nothing could have been surlier than Rupert's tone.

"Go and change your clothes."

Rupert stalked over to the trays.

"Is this all there is to eat?" He took a sandwich and ate it in a mouthful. "Damn, no mustard." Then he glanced at Riley who was eating a large sandwich. He walked over and pulled a bell-rope.

"What are you about?" said Augustus angrily.

Robert appeared. He had not expected a second summons and was neither clean nor correctly dressed.

"Bring me," said Rupert, "a couple of beef sandwiches with mustard, if that's all we're allowed to eat in this Godforsaken place. And a glass of beer."

"Yes, sir," said Robert, grinning approval. As he retreated, Augustus called:

"Robert!"

"Yes, sir?"

"You will bring nothing." He turned to Rupert who was close behind him. "If you want to eat like a servant, go and eat in the kitchen. Or better still, go and eat in the pigsty."

Rupert turned very red. He was much too young to keep his temper in such circumstances. Conversation throughout the room had ceased.

"Shut up," said Rupert, "you old fool!"

"Leave the room!" said Augustus.

"Everybody knows you're cracked," said Rupert backing towards the door. "You're the talk of the neighbourhood. You make us all look fools, with all this Georgian tomfoolery. You ought to see a doctor."

"Leave this house! And don't come back."

A woman's voice—Roger thought it was Dulcibella's— said, "Augustus!" But Rupert still retreated. His last shot was:

"Don't worry: you'll soon have the place to yourself. I'm the first, that's all."

Augustus stepped forward, but before he could strike Rupert, as he seemed to intend, the door was pulled to with a slam.

Conversation was resumed.

Roger, watching from the sofa where he still sat with Cornelia, thought that the effect was like that of mechanical figures which suddenly stop and as suddenly resume their motions when the clockwork or whatever it may be is started again. He turned to Cornelia.

"You were saying?"

"I told you Rupert hates Augustus. Now you see why."

"I have been learning a good deal within the last few hours."

"And what does your learning amount to?"

"I think Augustus—your father—is a lightning-defier."

V

Roger, looking back afterwards, could not remember anything remarkable about the rest of that day.

In the afternoon the three archæologists walked about on the terrace and on the lawn, smoking their pipes and saying little. Nobody else appeared until mid-afternoon, when from the outside of the house they saw Robert going round pulling down blinds and drawing curtains across the ground-floor windows. On the upper floor a woman was doing the same in the bedrooms. Soon the house wore its odd deserted aspect, as it had when they came, as of a place whose owners were away. They knew that behind those curtains and blinds the lights were lit, but they could not see these from outside because the sun was too bright.

At four o'clock Martin left them to go, he said, and make some plans and sketches from the particulars he had taken that morning on the site they had inspected; he also said he would not come down again, because presumably they were expected to be ready to dine at five as before.

At four fifteen Riley and Roger went upstairs to prepare themselves for the drawing-room ordeal.

At four forty-five they all assembled in the drawing-room as before: Augustus in his fancy dress, to which he seemed to have added a few touches, and the ladies in their high-waisted evening dresses and long gloves. The room was lit by the crystal chandelier, and there was conversation of a stilted kind, but no drinks. The people were the same as before except that Rupert was absent. The children were brought in for a moment and taken out again. Roger again spoke to Dulcibella but was stopped by a warning look in her eyes: old Mrs. Gale was near.

At a few minutes to five dinner was announced by Robert who wore his white coat. The rest of the evening passed according to Augustus's plan: after dinner a rather longer pause over the port wine and some very stiff talk about politics. Nothing personal was discussed, and there was no argument even on impersonal topics, because, although Augustus had said some preposterous things about the lower and even the middle classes to which the archæologists belonged, he appeared to take it for granted that they agreed with him—that all "gentlemen" held the same views—and they kept silent.

When they joined the ladies, tea was brought in, and a table for cards was placed for old Mrs. Gale, the Professor and two others. When Roger saw that one of these was to be Dulcibella he, too, decided to play, in the hope of being able to exchange looks with her and an occasional pressure of the foot, and to get out of the awful boredom the evening seemed to promise.

They were playing a game called "Speculation" of which he did not know the rules. He was pretending to listen to the confusing explanations of the other three when there was a stir at the back of the room.

The card-players looked round.

Augustus put down his cup, and with a hand above his heart hurried out of the room.

"He's ill!" said Dulcibella, going to the door. "He's ill!" cried Cornelia, leaving the table and hurrying after him.

She and Dulcibella met before the door, which Augustus had managed to close behind him.

When the door was opened by one of them, the rest of the party, crowding forward, saw Augustus lying on the floor in the hall. He was rolling about, evidently in pain. They heard him gasp: "God grant me patience!"

Coming down the stairs was Rupert with a suitcase in his hand. He paused to say contemptuously: "What's the matter with him?"

Someone—Cornelia or Dulcibella—said: "Get the doctor."

"Not I," said Rupert. "Get him yourself." He pushed past them and went out through the front door.

Old Mrs. Gale was kneeling at Augustus's head ineffectually trying to mop his brow with a very small handkerchief as he rolled to and fro, and wailing:

"Won't someone help? My poor boy! My poor boy!"

Riley said to Roger: "Can't *you* do something?"

Roger said: "Better give him an emetic." He loosened Augustus's cravat. "Stand back, you people!" He murmured to Riley: "He's pretty bad. Carry him to his room. We must get a doctor. I'll go."

He ran off, wishing he had his Vespa.

But before the doctor arrived, Augustus was dead.

2

The rest of the story was soon told. The emetic, salt and water, prepared by Robert and administered as best she could by Dulcibella, had had the desired effect. They had carried him to his room and put him to bed, but after about ten minutes he had rolled his eyes, shuddered and died.

"Did he say anything?" asked the doctor as he snapped his case to. "Anything articulate?"

Cornelia and Dulcibella looked at each other as if not sure whether they ought to give away Augustus's last words.

"Come on!" said the doctor irritably. "You were alone with him. There'll have to be a p.m. and an inquest. What, if anything, did he say?" He went to wash his hands at the basin in the bedroom. Augustus, marble-white, seemed still to prohibit liberties.

"He said—" began Cornelia, and stopped.

"He said," began Dulcibella and finished boldly:

"'Joan, my beloved, I am coming to you.'"

The doctor looked round: "Was that the name of his first wife?"

"No," said Cornelia. "My mother's name was Esther."

The doctor, a tubby little man called Jones, came towards them as he wiped his hands.

"Who was this Joan?" he said. "Do you know?"

"Yes," said Dulcibella. "We know."

"You're the second wife?" said the inquisitive doctor.

Dulcibella said: "I *was* the second wife."

"Oh. I see." The doctor was embarrassed. "Then I won't trouble you further. You'll have to answer questions, I'm afraid."

"What about?"

"This is not a natural death. It looks like suicide. We shall know more after the post-mortem." He threw the towel on to the floor and left Augustus's widow and his daughter together.

3

The archæologists left at once and walked back to the hotel. Each carried his suitcase, and Roger carried three cases: one containing his clothes, and two small ones, easily carried in one hand, containing his first-aid equipment and his chemical reagents. He was very thoughtful. His silence at last brought the inevitable facetious comment.

"A penny for your thoughts," said Riley.

What were his thoughts? Nothing that he could tell Riley or Martin. Chief among them ranked his arrangement with Dulcibella, an arrangement which Augustus's death must cancel. Roger had not even tried to get a private word with Dulcibella before he left: she seemed extremely upset, and he understood that it would not do to speak to her now of personal concerns. He himself wanted to be alone, to have time to think out the results of what had happened: Dulcie's freedom, for instance. Had Augustus suspected anything? He had said something in the overheard quarrel, had said he was not so blind as he might seem, and had implied that someone—his mother—had warned him. But Roger did not believe that he himself was suspected. But might he not have brought suspicion on himself by the way in which he had leapt to Dulcibella's defence? Yet Augustus had gone on treating him normally throughout dinner.

But none of this could be discussed with Riley, or even with Martin. He wondered if Martin had made any progress with Cornelia. He doubted it. It seemed to him that he himself had spent more time with her than Martin had, and of course Martin was a very slow starter, that he knew. A short weekend was not enough. But it didn't matter because, of course, Cornelia too was now free.

His continued silence evoked another question from Riley: "I wonder what it was that Gale took?"

4

Before the bar closed that evening Roger was called out: a police officer wished to see him. Would he be so good as to come along to the police station? Superintendent Mallett would be obliged. Roger, without returning to the bar, went with the constable to the door, and then, disliking being seen in the company of a uniformed man, went off to get his Vespa.

When he got to the station he was shown into an office where Mallett, Dr. Jones, Dr. Fitzbrown and several other police officers were waiting for him. When they all turned to look at him, Roger felt nervous, though they seemed friendly. His nervousness had been coming on for the past couple of hours: it was due, he knew, to his consciousness of his relations with the dead man's wife. Would they, could they, find out what was surely, so far, a secret between him and Dulcibella? Could he trust Dulcibella? Could he trust himself, for that matter? Do not people who feel guilty—and Augustus's death had that effect on him—give themselves away?

It is hard to remember that other people do not know what one knows about oneself. One often hands them what they can't possibly find out. Roger faced the men who were now staring at him.

The Superintendent shook hands with him.

"Sit down, Mr. Royden. Sorry to trouble you. It's about this unfortunate affair of Augustus Gale. You were present when he died."

"Not when he *died*," said Roger boldly. "I and my two colleagues were present—among others—when Gale collapsed in the entrance-hall. They carried him up to his room, and I offered to fetch a doctor. He died, I believe, before the doctor came."

"That's so," said Dr. Jones. "He was dead when I arrived."

"It took you some time to reach the doctor's house?" said Mallett.

"Yes. I went as fast as I could. I ran all the way. I had no means of transport, and besides, I didn't know where to look for the doctor's house. I had to enquire when I reached the town."

"Why didn't you phone?" said Mallett.

"Phone?" said Roger. "There's no telephone at Geffrye House."

"No telephone? In a house so remote? In these times?"

"Geffrye House," said Roger solemnly, "is not of these times. There is no telephone. Augustus Gale did his best to keep out all modern inventions. But you surely know that: it's the key to the whole affair."

"What affair?" snapped Mallett.

"Gale's death," said Roger.

"That," said Mallett, "will be for the Coroner to decide. There will be an inquest on Tuesday morning at eleven. You will be wanted there, Mr. Royden—and your colleagues. But you will receive official intimation. We have sent for you now to ask you something which may help us. You are an analytical chemist?"

"I am."

"Attached to the archæological party now excavating the mosaics near Geffrye House, under the auspices of the Romano-British Society?"

"Yes."

"Your duty is to analyse substances unearthed in these excavations?"

"Yes—when I can."

"And for this purpose you carry with you certain equipment—chemical reagents and so on."

"Of course," said Roger. "But what is this? It sounds to me like an inquisition. What's the idea?"

"Don't get excited," said Mallett. "You will certainly be asked to answer all these questions—under oath—at the inquest. But—"

Dr. Fitzbrown stepped forward. He was a tall, pleasant-looking man with black curly hair. He said soothingly:

"The Superintendent is only asking you questions because that may help to make the inquest go more easily and quickly." He turned to Mallett: "I say, hadn't you better come to the point?"

Mallett said:

"I think perhaps Dr. Jones had better take over."

Jones said:

"The point is, Royden, the p.m. shows that Gale died of a powerful dose of some kind of mercury poisoning. The police want to know where he got it. They've found nothing of the kind in the house, and they can't begin trying to trace the source, doing the round of chemists' shops and so on, until they know in what form the poor devil chose to take the mercury."

Roger started and gripped the seat of his chair. He looked the picture of guilt.

"Wait a minute," he said.

Jones stepped forward inquisitively.

"Did you have any mercurial salt among your reagents?"

"Not among my reagents," said Roger.

"Where, then?"

"In my first-aid kit. I took it everywhere with me. It had become a habit: I often had to do minor surgical operations like lancing boils, taking splinters out, and so on. Once I took a tooth out," he said proudly, adding with ingrained honesty: "It was loose."

"Rather more than first aid," said Jones. "Go on. I think I see daylight."

"So I had to have something to sterilise instruments."

"And for that you used——"

"Biniodide of mercury."

"Old-fashioned," said Jones. "So you had biniodide of mercury with you? Where was it? Was it accessible?"

"Was it accessible to others?" resumed Mallett.

"It was in a small case. I call it my first-aid case, but it is rather more than that, as you say. I have built it up in the light of my own experience with archæological expeditions abroad as well as in this country."

"You had this biniodide of mercury," said Mallett, making a careful note of the name, "in what you call your first-aid case. Was this case open?"

"Open?" said Roger. He repeated the word in a stupid manner because he had been struck by a thought which disconcerted him and he wanted to gain time.

"Locked or unlocked?" said Mallett impatiently.

"It was usually locked, but it may have been unlocked. I'm not sure, but I think it was unlocked——" He was going on to explain why, but Mallett interrupted:

"Then Gale could have got at the contents. Where did you keep the case?"

"The case was in my bedroom at Geffrye House."

"Was the bottle labelled?"

"Yes."

"Was it labelled 'Poison'?"

"Yes." Roger was glad to be able to say this: he had always conscientiously stuck red "poison" labels on any of his bottles that needed them.

"In what form was this poison? Liquid?"

"Oh no. I carried it in the usual form: tablets to be dissolved in water when required."

"Do you know the strength of the tablets?"

"Not exactly," said Roger. "They were made up to be dissolved in a pint of water, as a disinfectant. They weren't made to be taken."

Mallett gave Jones an inquiring look.

"That's so," said Jones. "He wouldn't know the exact quantity in the made-up tablets. But they'd be highly toxic. And biniodide tablets suit our findings: potassium as well as mercury, y'know."

Mallett nodded.

"I don't think we need detain Mr. Royden any longer."

Roger got up, a trifle too eagerly.

"Do you mean to say Gale got into my room and pinched one of these tablets?"

"That," said Mallett, "is for the Coroner to decide, after weighing the evidence. We shall see."

Roger moved towards the door, glad to get away but aware of an unsatisfactory feeling, a desire to ask questions, but without knowing what these questions could be.

Dr. Jones said:

"And if I were you, I'd leave surgery—even minor surgery—to qualified men. In fact, the general view is, y'know, there's no such thing as *minor* surgery. Then you could put things like mercury salts in the fire. All *you* need is boiling water, anyway."

"All right," said Roger, irritated.

When he stepped out of the police station, he was aware of the sweet night air, in which the scents of wallflowers and seaweed were blended. But he was not soothed. He was puzzled, apprehensive, completely miserable.

5

After he had gone Mallett turned to the two doctors.

"Well? What are we going to make of that?"

"It's clear where Gale got the tablet or tablets, anyway," said Jones.

"Yes: we can wash out the trek round the chemists' shops, thank goodness."

"There's a missing link, you know," said Fitzbrown quietly.

"Yes, I know," said Mallett. "I was thinking that. How did Gale know that the tablets were in Royden's case?"

Nobody answered till Jones said dubiously: "Royden must have let Gale see the case. The bottle was labelled 'Poison'. Funny he didn't keep it locked."

"Oh, that's nothing," said Mallett. "It's easy enough to get a key to unlock an ordinary case."

"But we don't know it was an ordinary case."

"We must satisfy ourselves about that," said Mallett. He signed to one of his men: "Collins, go round to the Imperial and ask Mr. Royden to give you what he calls his first-aid case."

The constable saluted and went.

"How did this man Royden strike you?" said the Superintendent.

"Nervous—and shifty," said Jones, who always thought the worst of everybody, and treated all human beings, including his own patients, as guilty of some unspecified crime unless they were seriously and obviously ill.

Dr. Fitzbrown belonged to the class of doctors who follow the ancient Hippocratic rule that medicine is one of the branches of humanitarianism.

"Nervous," he admitted, "and ill at ease. But what do you expect? He had to face a semicircle of strangers who appeared to be accusing him of something."

"We accused him of nothing," said Mallett quietly.

"Not in so many words. But you were hinting at—"

"At what?" said Jones aggressively.

"Well, officiousness for one thing. And carelessness for another."

"He didn't seem sure," reflected Mallett, "whether the case was locked or unlocked. What he said suggested to me that he usually kept it locked but had unlocked it recently for some reason or other. I meant to go into that but something diverted me. We'll have to have him back, I'm afraid."

6

They had no need to send for Roger.

When Collins returned with the suitcase Roger was with him. He was in a high state of indignation.

"Look here," he said as he burst into the room with the constable. "What's this all about? What right have you—"

Mallett stopped him.

"We have every right, I assure you, to take all the steps we think necessary in inquiring into a violent death. We have no right to detain *you*. Go if you wish. But I wanted to ask you a few more questions, and I think you'd do well to answer."

"Gale's death has nothing to do with me."

"It has, in so far as he appears to have taken a tablet from your case." Mallett indicated, without touching, the case which Collins had placed before him on the table. "Open it," he said.

Roger stepped forward, but Mallett waved him back. Collins drew on his white gloves and released the catches.

"The case is unlocked," said Mallett superfluously. "Is this how you found it?"

"Yes."

"With the lid fastened down?"

"Yes."

Mallett said:

"Then Gale's fingerprints should be all over it. Take it to the lab. and have it tested." He turned to Roger. "Did you at any time show it to Gale?"

"No. Why should I?"

"Never mind why. Did you or did you not?"

"I did not."

"Did you show it to anyone else?"

"Show what?"

"The case."

"Everybody must have seen it as I went in."

Mallett said irritably: "The contents—did you show Gale, or anyone else, the contents?"

"I don't remember. I don't think so."

He remembered perfectly well and was dreading the question.

Dr. Jones stepped forward.

"Why don't you speak the truth?"

Dr. Fitzbrown intervened quietly:

"Yes, you'd do better to tell the truth. The Superintendent is suggesting that Gale must either have seen the bottle labelled 'Poison' or been told about it by someone else."

Roger looked relieved.

"I may have shown some of my kit to the ladies," he said.

"Go on," said Fitzbrown. "Ladies are proverbially curious."

"I think I showed it when I arrived to members of the family."

"Why?"

"Miss Gale—or possibly Mrs. Gale—showed me to my room. One of them remarked on the number of my cases —I had three— so I showed the two cases that were for work: the chemical equipment and the so-called first-aid case."

"And after that you didn't lock the case."

"Evidently not. I don't remember."

They stared at him in such a way that he knew they didn't want him any more.

"Can I have my case?" he said.

"After the inquest," said Mallett.

Roger was forced to go.

7

The next morning, about noon, a taxi drove to the police station. Out of it stepped a sprightly man with a white beard; he handed out an old lady who got up the steps without waiting for him. By the time he caught up with her she was being shown into Superintendent Mallett's office.

"I am Mrs. Gale—Augustus Gale's mother," she said, taking the chair offered to her, and looking like a toad on a toadstool. "I wish to speak to you privately. I—"

The police constable was about to shut the door when the old lady's escort nimbly stepped in.

"I," he said, "am Professor Bose. I have something to say to you about the late Augustus Gale."

"Please wait outside," said Mallett. "I shall be glad to see you as soon as possible." He signalled to the constable. "Show the Professor to the waiting-room. You can then stay on the other side of the door."

"Now, Superintendent," said Mrs. Gale, when the other two had gone, "you are investigating the death of my son, who appears to have taken poison. You will be told some very strange tales about him. There will be an attempt to show, among other things, that he was insane. I have come to put you on the right track."

"Thank you, ma'am," said Mallett with a bow.

"He was not insane," she went on. "There has never been any insanity in our family. But in these times, if anyone deviates at all from what people choose to regard as the norm, he is considered—labelled—insane. I have come here to protect my son's memory from such a stigma."

"*Is* it a stigma?" said Mallett. "Surely it's better if there's a verdict of suicide, that the man should be labelled insane rather than as one that took his own life deliberately, which, according to our law, is a crime—a crime which, if the subject should recover, is liable to severe penalties."

"You needn't explain the law to me, sir," snapped Mrs. Gale. "I know all about it. It is in many respects idiotic and greatly in need of reform. But I haven't come here to discuss that with you.

You're paid to administer the law as you find it. I pity you. I haven't lived to be over eighty without recognising its many anomalies."

"The Coroner usually adds, 'temporary insanity'," Mallett reminded her. "It's better, surely, than the old *felo de se*."

"There's no such thing as temporary insanity," said Mrs. Gale sharply. "A man's sane, or he's mad. My son was not mad. He was, perhaps, according to modern standards, eccentric—though *I* don't think it eccentric to worship the great. I will not have him labelled insane—not even temporarily insane. He has four children, two by his first wife, a grown-up son and a daughter of marriageable age; two young children, a boy and a girl, by his second wife." Her tone and expression conveyed quite clearly to Mallett a dislike of the second marriage, either because of dislike of the second Mrs. Augustus Gale or because of a disapproval of second marriages. "I want the reputations of these children to be preserved from the terrible stigma of having had a father who was insane."

"Nothing can protect them against the knowledge that their father committed suicide," said Mallett; and then, hastily recollecting himself, "that is, if he really did, if the Coroner's verdict—"

"Of course he did!" snapped Mrs. Gale. "We all saw him."

"You *saw* him?" Mallett leaned across the desk. "You know in what form he took the poison?"

Mrs. Gale made exclamations of impatience. "He drank his cup of tea with us all in the drawing-room as usual. We always have tea after dinner: it was a rule of Augustus's, for reasons—But never mind that, yet. He drank his tea and hurried out of the room. He collapsed in the hall. We got him to bed. One of the young men staying with us went for the doctor. But Augustus died before the doctor came."

"You were with him?"

"Yes."

"Did he say anything?"

"He was delirious. He said nothing relevant—nothing about taking poison."

"He knew he was dying?"

"Yes. He said something that implied that he expected to join—others."

"But you didn't *see* him put anything into his cup?"

"How could I? I wasn't watching. I never pour out tea, naturally; my son's wife does that, or his daughter. But it stands to reason he must have put the poison into the tea, doesn't it—since he fell ill immediately afterwards."

"It stands to reason," said Mallett, "that the poison was in the tea. Tell me, Mrs. Gale, do you know in what form the poison was administered?"

"I've told you," said the old lady as snappily as ever, "I saw nothing. I was at the other end of the room. I was already sitting at the card-table. I had begun to play our usual game of 'Speculation' with the Professor and two others. We always do this after dinner. It's such a long evening when you dine at five. I've never quite got used to it."

"Who were the other two at the table?" interrupted Mallett.

"One of them was the young man—Roger Something—who went for the doctor. I remember him because he didn't know the game and we had to waste a great deal of time explaining the rules. I was thinking, 'He may be good at this archæology, but he's not very clever at anything else: the rules are quite simple.' And then I wondered. You see, my daughter-in-law also was at our table, and I had heard—"

"Who was the other player, did you say?"

"An Irishman whose name I forget. He was one of the visitors too. I don't know why Augustus invited them. He doesn't like visitors as a rule. But perhaps——"

"So you were at the table with the Professor and the two young men, when——"

Mrs. Gale described Augustus's sudden exit and collapse.

"But," she said, "you know all that. What I'm here to bring home to you is that there must *not* be a verdict of insanity, temporary or otherwise, because it would not be the truth."

"Why are you so sure? Naturally, as his mother——"

"Nothing to do with my being his mother, sir. It so happens I know his motive."

"You do!"

"By accident I learnt it. I overheard his wife talking to the young man Roger. He was making love to her."

To Mallett this expression meant something which could not be carried out in the drawing-room or in company. "Will you be more specific?" he said.

"For some time my son and his second wife—she has the ridiculous name of Dulcibella—have not been living a normal married life."

"They quarrel?"

"No, sir. Not openly: my son would never have done that. But they had separate rooms. My son always wanted a large family, as in the good old days."

"Hem!" was Mallett's only comment.

"The evening before last, I overheard the young man Roger proposing to Dulcibella that she should elope with him—leave her husband. They were even discussing what was to be done with the children, and she was planning a monstrous piece of wickedness—she was not only going to desert him, but she was going to take the children too. Since then there have been other incidents. As soon as I saw my son alone, I told him."

"You *told* him?"

"Of course. I wished him to prevent such a scandalous thing, if only for the sake of the children."

"When did you tell him?"

"I went to him between dinner and the tea-drinking. He was in his room. I told him what I had seen and heard, and what Professor Bose had said also."

"What did your husband say?"

"He expressed disbelief. He pretended not to take me seriously."

"Do you remember anything he said, word for word?"

"Yes. He did say, rather strangely, I thought: 'Why should I care? Let her go if she wishes. I have that of which no living man can rob me.'"

"What did he mean?"

"I do not know. But I fear that the revelation was too much for him. Even if he cares nothing for Dulcibella, which may well be—she never suited him and he made a great mistake in marrying her—my son was a man of very fixed ideas, a man of great dignity of character and decorum of behaviour. He could never have faced the awful scandal, the publicity that attends such things nowadays: his private life, his idiosyncrasies, exposed to the world! Reporters, photographers—"

"I'm afraid," said Mallett, "you will have to endure a certain amount of publicity as things are. Your son's action will have brought that on you. But," he added gently, "don't let it trouble you too much: it's one of the conditions of our present age. And it soon passes. They forget you and hurry off to something else."

"No reporter will be admitted to Geffrye House," said old Mrs. Gale, folding up her very thin long mouth, "if I can prevent it."

Mallett said no more on this head. She was a formidable old lady, but he doubted if even she could keep reporters out of Geffrye House: there was so much to be reported, it seemed.

"You *wish* to give evidence at the inquest tomorrow?"

"I do."

"I know you have been summoned, but you could get an exemption, I dare say, if you wished. It will be something of an ordeal for you—"

"I care only to protect my son's reputation."

"In that case—" Mallett stood up.

8

Professor Bose came trippingly into the room.

"I thought," he said, holding out a thin, veined hand and leaving it limply in Mallett's large red one, "I ought to come along and give you the background of this case. It is very relevant."

"Are you related to the deceased?" said Mallett.

Professor Bose walked up and down the room.

"No. But I soon should have been—by marriage. With Gale's consent, I was engaged to marry his daughter Cornelia. Poor Gale! We were the greatest of friends and cronies; I suppose I was the only one of them who could handle him."

"Was that difficult?"

"Very. Ask any member of his household. Poor Gale was not quite right in the head, you know. He was yet another instance of a clever, sensitive, imaginative man who can't face up to life, as his last action proves. I suppose the verdict will be 'suicide during temporary insanity'?"

"I can't anticipate the verdict, sir. But you think he was insane, do you? You don't think it was just momentary disturbance?"

"Of course he was insane!"

"His mother won't have it. She came here expressly to tell me that he was sane."

"His mother! What use is a mother's evidence? Old Mrs. Gale worshipped her son, naturally, but it doesn't follow she understood him."

"Perhaps not. Would you care to tell me—off the record, of course—what makes you think Gale was mad?"

"Don't you know?"

"No," said Mallett, "otherwise I wouldn't have asked you to tell me, would I? I have no time to waste."

"I thought everybody knew that Augustus Gale was an anachronism."

"A what?"

"A man trying to live in a time other than his own. He bought Geffrye House because it was the birthplace of the famous Regency playwright, Joan Farmer, and her home for many years till she grew up and went to London. She returned there to die in 1817."

Mallett suppressed a yawn: his green eyes bulged with the effort.

"Gale," went on the Professor, without noticing as he paced the room, "not only restored Geffrye House and made it fit for present occupation, he arranged there in the basement a very fine collection of Farmer relics: must be worth quite a lot." He paused at this great thought and sucked the rim of his spectacles, which were pince-nez on a black ribbon. "He has left the house and the collection to his mother for her lifetime and after that to me. He does not want the collection to be dispersed: after our deaths it is to go to the nation."

"So you can't dispose of any of it?"

"No. As I see it, it is a burden, not a bequest of value. You see, he has left no money for its upkeep. I doubt if the estate would have run to that. Therefore, when his mother dies—and she's over eighty—I shall have a white elephant on my hands."

"You can decline it."

"Yes—but I feel I must accept it for Gale's sake. I was the one he always turned to for help and advice in these matters."

"You are an antiquarian?"

"I have specialised in the late Georgian period, and Gale always called me in when he wanted to choose furniture or arrange the life of the house. You see," he went on as if explaining to a very stupid child, "he was so devoted to the memory of Joan Farmer that he wished to live, as closely as possible, as she lived: he wished the house to be run on early-nineteenth-century lines."

"No drainage?" Mallett smiled. "No electricity?"

"He didn't go as far as that. He allowed drainage of a sort, and even electricity, though the fittings were as much like the old ones as he could acquire. He spent a great deal more than he could afford on magnificent crystal chandeliers—but the ladies, the second Mrs. Gale and his daughter Cornelia, my fiancée, wouldn't have candles in them because of the mess. Augustus had to be got to realise that the house was not full of servants as it would have been in Joan Farmer's day."

"What servants had they?"

"They were lucky to have a cook, a part-time maid of some sort, and a man-of-all-work, who had to wait at table as well as carry coal and chop wood and clean shoes and so on. Gale flew into frightful rages if anything he disliked came to his notice. So the ladies got round the problem by dressing Robert up in different coats according to his various duties." The Professor gave a dry laugh. "How the fellow stood it, I don't know. He must have been the cook's lover, I suppose. That didn't matter so long as Gale didn't know."

"He flew into rages on small provocation. Anything else?"

"This craze of his—this period craze—had been getting worse lately."

"Really? Can you give me an example?"

"When I first knew him, ten years ago, his dress was more normal than it is now."

"Will you explain?"

"One of his foibles was to dine at five, as would have been customary in Joan Farmer's day. He used to dress for dinner in a very dark-blue coat and a cravat, and as he wore his hair in those long lines on the cheeks, known, I believe, by the vulgar as sideboards, he had himself a Georgian air. This was usual with him; we had all got used to it, anyway. But I noticed, on Saturday night, he was in full costume, with light-coloured breeches and shoes with buckles. This was a change: he had never gone so far before, though he had always insisted on the period evening dresses for the ladies—a pretty custom, I thought."

"This was on Saturday night," said Mallett. "What about Sunday—yesterday?"

"During the day when he went to church and afterwards for a walk through the grounds with those young men, he was normally dressed. But when he came into the drawing-room before dinner, he had his fancy costume on again, and it seemed to me he looked much more like a Georgian gentleman than ever. I wondered why he was carrying the masquerade to such lengths, and whether he was trying to impress the visitors."

"You mean the three members of the archæological party who were spending the Saturday and Sunday nights at Geffrye House?"

The Professor nodded shortly. His manner clearly expressed that he disliked the intrusion of the archaeologists.

"I understand," said Mallett, "that Geffrye House, besides being of historic interest to lovers of literature, has also recently been the scene of another discovery?"

"Oh yes," said the Professor casually, "the Roman mosaics. Most of them are outside the wall. They seem very inferior work to me: in fact, Gale said to me at dinner on Sunday— But I advise you to ask the young men themselves."

"I will," said Mallett.

9

When Riley came into the room in response to Mallett's message, Mallett said to him bluntly:

"All this is quite off the record, Mr. Riley. Tell me, did *you* think Augustus Gale was mad?"

Riley considered. Then he answered in a more richly Irish voice than usual:

"It depends on what you mean by 'mad'. The term is relative."

"I know," said Mallett patiently. "But would you from any point of view have described Gale as mad?"

"*I* wouldn't," said Riley promptly. "But you might. I'm an Irishman. In my country Gale wouldn't have been considered mad at all. He *was*, perhaps, a little peculiar, but there's nothing mad about living in the past. Lots of people do it and get away with it, even in England. People like myself are paid to try to do it."

"But surely," said Mallett, "there's a difference between *your* work, which is an attempt to recreate the past by scientific means—"

"Plus imagination," said Riley, "if any."

Mallett continued: "—and trying to *live* in some past era."

"There is a difference," said Riley after some thought, "but the nearer the true archæologist can get to *living* in the past, the better he is."

"But," said Mallett irritably, "the man was recreating the past, not in his imagination but in fact. I mean, he was recreating, concretely, the life of the early nineteenth century as far as he could."

"Well," said Riley, "there are worse times in which one could have lived."

"No drainage?" said Mallett, to whom sanitation was of the greatest importance.

"My dear sir," said Riley, "there must be a great many places in what used to be correctly called the United Kingdom where there are no drains! Some of them, maybe, are not a hundred miles from here. One of the remarks of my fellow countryman, Bernard Shaw, which was true as well as shocking, was that many of the inhabitants of Britain are living as they did in the days of King Alfred."

"Fewer and fewer," argued Mallett, "and not the—"

"Not the gentry?" said Riley with a smile. "No, when they want a bit of nature and some good food, they come to Ireland or cross the Channel. But you didn't get me here to discuss sanitation."

"I wanted your opinion on Gale's mental state."

"I hardly knew him."

"Coming in from outside," said Mallett, "you were perhaps a better judge than his own family."

"Do they think he was mad?" Riley opened his eyes. "They suffered from his caprices, but as they didn't live in the Georgian era they could have left."

"One of them," said Mallett, "was planning to, apparently." He stopped, remembering that one of the eloping couple would have been a member of Riley's party. "So you say he wasn't mad."

"I didn't say that: I said I didn't know. I said it wasn't necessarily a sign of madness to try to live in another era. It depends which era."

"Mr. Riley, will you tell me—still off the record—a little about your work at Geffrye House, in so far as it concerned Gale?"

"There's nothing to tell," said Riley. "We did no work at Geffrye House because Gale wouldn't let us. Worse than that, he was destroying the Roman remains which happened to lie within his boundary-wall. Now in that, I feel, he may have been a little mad."

"Why did he refuse you his permission?"

"Because he had this thing about Joan Farmer, the Regency playwright. If we had started digging where we wanted, we would have been bound to remove part of a mound on which there had once been a summer-house in which this Joan Farmer used to write her plays."

"And that seems to you mad?"

"'A *little* mad', I said. We are all mad: we have this thing about Roman remains, Gale had it about Joan Farmer and her era, and our different madnesses clashed. That's all."

"That's what you mean to say at the inquest?"

"If I'm asked the same questions, yes. I don't think Gale was any more mad that many of his fellow creatures. What's madder than to sit all day watching two men hit a ball to and fro? Yet thousands of people do it every year at your Wimbledon."

"That's different."

"Of course it's different: it's a different craze—a different compulsion. Gale had a compulsion, but it wasn't imposed on him from outside, by his own age and time: it came from within. His psychology is most interesting. I used to do psychology before I got captivated by archæology. There's nothing odd in Gale's attitude to Joan Farmer. It is a simple case of hero-worship, only as the object of his admiration happened to be a woman. Gale's emotions were more deeply involved so that the poor fellow found himself in the uncomfortable position of being in love with a departed soul. Let's hope he'll meet her now: he has loved much, so his sin—the sin of despair —will be forgiven him." He crossed himself and remained for a moment silent with bowed head.

"He had a wife," remarked Mallett after a pause, "a *second* wife."

"That has nothing to do with it," said Riley, "except that it was very hard on her. A beautiful woman; one of my colleagues has fallen in love with her, and I think the lady responds. So that Gale's death is, in a way, a happy event, for him and her, as well as for us."

"In what way is it a happy event for you?"

"Because we shall, now that Gale is removed, have a good chance of getting permission to excavate the rest of our mosaic pavement, which is what we live for at present." He smiled. "You don't think *we're* mad to waste so much of our youth digging up a very inferior Roman pavement? No, because we're paid for it. That's sufficient reason for everything, isn't it? By the way, do you know who is the new owner of Geffrye House? It's all public and comes into force, a will I mean, as soon as a man dies, doesn't it? I must know, so that I can begin activating—seeing people and writing letters."

"I understand," said Mallett, "that the house is his mother's during her lifetime, but then it passes to Professor Bose, and after that to the National Trust."

"Good. I suppose the old lady will follow her son's ruling and not let us touch the mosaic. But if only she'll leave it alone, so that the thing is preserved— I'd better see her."

"If I were you," said Mallett, "I'd see the Professor. He may have some influence with the old lady. She might turn nasty towards *you*. But the Professor was in her son's confidence."

"Thank you: I'll do that." Riley stretched himself, yawned, and got up. "It's my job," he said, "and I shall do my best. But I don't really care a damn what happens to the mosaics—off the record, of course."

10

Mallett had a long talk with the two doctors and with his colleagues; when the Coroner arrived on Tuesday morning they had a conference. The result of all this was that it was decided that the inquest should not be adjourned for further inquiries: no good could be done and it would be better for a verdict to be recorded forthwith.

It seemed so clear that Augustus had poisoned himself, and the police do not waste time on fruitless investigations; there is plenty of crime in the world without inventing it, and there was no evidence that anyone had caused Augustus's death but himself.

VI

The inquest passed off without any surprises.

The witnesses gave the evidence that had been expected of them: the pathologist, Dr. Jones, gave evidence that the deceased had died through taking a fatal dose of some mercury compound. Dr. Fitzbrown, who had assisted at the post-mortem, corroborated this. The whole Gale family was present except, of course, the two young children: Mrs. Gale, Mrs. Augustus Gale, Miss Cornelia Gale, Rupert Gale. The outsiders were: Professor Bose, prospective husband of Cornelia, the three archæologists, the servant Robert and Augustus's secretary Miss Smith.

The Gales sat together in a family party. They looked odd, and they looked ill-assorted as if they were strangers to one another. The women especially looked odd because of their hats. Roger had never seen any of them before wearing a hat and he was not aware of what troubled him. Old Mrs. Gale wore a hat that stood high on her head, one she had not renewed for many years. Cornelia wore a wide-brimmed hat. Dulcibella's hat was hardly to be distinguished from her black hair, but when Roger had seen her before she had either been bare-headed or had had only a scarf thrown over her head. They were all called upon to testify, but none of them was allowed to say all that he or she thought.

The Coroner summed up sympathetically.

"We have heard," he said, "from unexceptionable witnesses, of the deceased's peculiar attachment to the Georgian way of life. This might not be considered odd, but he carried it to extremes, making all his family observe the same reverence towards the past, sometimes to their evident discomfort, though none of them has complained. Still, to live within such restrictions must have been irksome in the present century."

He went on to speak of the medical evidence and to praise the doctors, one of whom, Dr. Jones, had been released earlier in the proceedings, for the clarity and succinctness of their testimony. "It was, perhaps, a little unfortunate," he said with a glance under bushy eyebrows at Roger, "that Mr. Roydon, one of the guests, had with him an attaché-case containing a bottle of tablets, one of which constituted a fatal poison, and that he left this case unlocked in his room. He has explained to us the fortuitous steps by which this circumstance arose, and I must say he has spoken with complete frankness and has made no attempt to defend any carelessness one might think was involved. His explanation has been corroborated by the two ladies, the widow and the daughter of the deceased, who both say that they pressed Mr. Royden to show them the contents of the case and have both shown an altruistic desire to take upon themselves any blame." He smiled. "If one were a philosopher, one might perhaps say that the episode reveals the feminine character in two of its most familiar aspects: curiosity and self-sacrifice." He looked down his nose to give time for the appreciation of the mild jest. He included one of these in most of his disquisitions and they were a great boon not only to the reporters, who regularly included them in their accounts, but also to sub-editors, who used them as headlines. "However that may be, I do not wish to emphasise this point unduly. I am sure that Mr.

Royden, profiting by this unhappy experience, will take care to lock his case in future."

He paused and looked round over his reading glasses.

"We can therefore deduce that the deceased took the tablets from Mr. Royden's so-called first-aid case. How he found them we cannot hope to know. It is possible that one of the ladies mentioned the matter to him, though neither of them remembers doing so. The case was open. The bottle was labelled 'Poison'—a very proper precaution on Mr. Royden's part but which as it happened caught the deceased's eye and directed him where to go. He took one or more of the tablets from the bottle, and appears to have administered them to himself by mouth in a cup of tea, it being one of the Georgian customs instituted by him to drink tea after dinner. In the late eighteenth and early nineteenth century, it seems, it was quite usual in upper—or perhaps upper middle-class—circles, to dine at the early hour of five o'clock, and later to drink tea or coffee and pass the evening in musical entertainment and in playing cards."

He coughed. The inflection of his voice suggested that he was sorry for Augustus's family, obliged to fall in with his whims. No radio, no television. Nothing but homemade music and obsolete card games! And dinner at five! Barbarous! This was exactly what the Coroner was thinking, except that he himself disliked television and had refused his own sons' and daughters' eager request that he should buy a television set. He liked to live in his own time, which was the early twentieth century, not in the mid-twentieth century and certainly not in the early nineteenth. He went on:

"The question of motive now arises. The deceased left no note for me or for any member of his family. Enquiries have failed to elicit any obvious motive. Mr. Gale was not in any financial difficulties, nor was he, so far as his family knew, troubled by any worries, reasonable or groundless, about his health. We can therefore only suppose, on the evidence before us, that his act was the result of a sudden impulse. He was a man of sudden impulses, as we have seen. He was also a histrionic type, as we know from his dress. Whatever he did he liked to do before an audience: otherwise we might wonder why he should choose to do what he did in public.

"Now I must say at once that I have not been able, on the evidence, to find grounds for believing Mr. Gale was insane. His predilection for the Georgian way of life was odd and oddly expressed; but it was not insanity, not certifiable insanity in the medical or legal sense; that is to say, no two doctors would have been prepared to say that he must be deprived of his independence and his liberty. But I think we have had evidence which proves that he was unstable. His secretary, Miss Smith, speaks of sudden attacks of rage: but she admits that these by themselves might be regarded as no more than a rather autocratic man's irritation, excessive perhaps, but not entirely causeless. Many a business man might be certified as insane if an attack of irritation at a typing mistake, for instance, is regarded as evidence." He smiled his self-conscious, prim smile, which meant, "Reporters take note." "And Miss Smith admits that she did sometimes make mistakes or fail to understand Mr. Gale's meaning, but that on the whole they agreed perfectly well together as employer and employee. We must accept this, because obviously if he had not been basically satisfied with Miss Smith's work he would have dismissed her, and if she had been tried too far by an unreasonable temper, she would have left him and sought another situation.

"From several sources we have evidence of irritable behaviour: Mr. Riley has testified to having seen the deceased unreasonably angry with one of his children, and to an unpleasant scene involving the two young children and their mother. Mrs. Gale, widow of the deceased, has reluctantly corroborated this evidence. The deceased's behaviour in this instance cannot, I think, be regarded as quite normal. It is unusual for a man in Mr. Gale's position to speak roughly to his wife, and strike his children, in the presence of strangers, or indeed in the presence of any onlookers. Mr. Riley has put forward the suggestion that Mr. Gale did not know that he, Mr. Riley, and the other two guests, were onlookers; he has also suggested as an explanation of the deceased's extreme irritability— an irritability which perhaps blinded him to the presence of witnesses—that he had, before this incident, been showing the archæologists that part of the Roman mosaic which lay in his own grounds, and making it clear to them that he would not allow them to continue their investigations there. This, says Mr. Riley, may have started up a train of resentment which exploded later on the innocent objects that met him. This ingenious explanation, for which we are grateful to Mr. Riley, may be true; but it still to my mind—I am not a psychologist in the modern sense—suggests a lack of balance which is not normal. In other words, the deceased was a man abnormally liable to act on impulse.

"We have also had evidence of a scene which took place between the deceased and his eldest son, Rupert, on Sunday afternoon. It appears from Mr. Rupert Gale's evidence that he strongly disapproved of and resisted his father's attempt to impose Georgian ways of life on his household. On this particular day he had himself gone out shooting in the morning and returned just before what in most people's houses would be the time for luncheon. Under Augustus Gale's régime only wine was served at this time. When Rupert Gale walked into the drawing-room where the guests were assembled, he had not bothered to change into suitable clothes.

Both son and father were irritated, Rupert Gale says, because he dislikes shooting and only shoots because his father wishes it— it was the chief outdoor sport for men in the Georgian era—and because there was nothing to eat. Rupert Gale ordered the servant to bring him a sandwich. The father countermanded the order, using somewhat offensive expressions. Rupert Gale says that he was used to being roughly spoken to, but not in front of company. There were three strange young men present on this occasion, for one of whom—Mr. Riley—his father had ordered a sandwich. He answered back with some unusually violent expression and his father ordered him out of the room— and even out of the house.

"This was a sad incident to occur between father and son so soon before the former's death, and the son very naturally regrets it. But I think it is one more small piece of evidence that the deceased was not in a normal frame of mind. Like the mosaic pavement of which we have heard so much, these pieces of evidence, small and meaningless in themselves, build up a clear and consistent picture.

"Lastly, I come to the most important piece of evidence on this head, that of the employee, Robert Brook. One of the chief difficulties of trying to live a nineteenth-century life in twentieth-century England is the lack of staff. Thus Robert Brook, who has been employed in the Gale household since he was a boy of fourteen, has come, at the age of twenty-five, to be a sort of Poo-Bah—general factotum. Amongst his duties was that of butler. He has described how, on Saturday evening, after dinner, when the ladies had left, the deceased made a scene over some port wine; Brook says that the deceased's manner frightened him, though he was used to such outbreaks. He says his master 'looked murderous', and that he thought he was going to strike him or throw something at him—that he, the deceased, had already thrown a glass of wine across the room. He, Brook, was so much alarmed by the deceased's threatening attitude that he did not stop even to sweep up the broken glass or wipe the wine off the wall and floor, but ran out of the room. This account is corroborated by the three guests, Mr. Riley, Mr. Royden and Mr. Praa, who of course were present when their host threw the glass across the room. They say that Mr. Gale was angry because Brook had brought the wrong port. Mr. Royden and Mr. Praa say that they had tasted the port and could see nothing wrong with it. Mr. Riley, who claims to be more of a connoisseur, says that the port tasted like—to use his own words—'one of those filthy medicinal concoctions', and added that he thought Mr. Gale was quite justified in his anger, if we bear in mind Mr. Gale's attitude towards the graces of life, among which, Mr. Riley informs us, port wine of the best vintage must certainly be included."

There was a faint titter. The Coroner went on seriously:

"The anger may have been justified, especially in a connoisseur of wine entertaining guests. But was the action equally justified? Was it normal? Have we not all felt similar disappointments in matters of food and drink, but do we react by hurling our plates and glasses across rooms? I think not. And I think that a man who does so must be regarded as unstable, liable to impulsive actions which he cannot control. Thus, though the deceased was not insane, I think we may in the light of the evidence regard him as one the balance of whose mind was somewhat easily disturbed."

The Coroner dwelt for some time further on Augustus's well-known peculiarities of temper and ended: "I must make it clear that there is no evidence whatever that the deceased died by any hand but his own. His motive must remain a mystery: possibly it arose from his over-fertile imagination." He recorded a verdict of "Suicide while the balance of his mind was disturbed", on Augustus Gale.

After the Coroner had left, the family filed out, watched sympathetically by the rest of the onlookers. When they reached the steps outside, the photographers, forbidden to function within, began snapping the grief-stricken widow, mother and daughter. Roger watched Dulcibella intently, hoping to get her to give him a glance. But she did not: she was pale and composed, and though she had to follow old Mrs. Gale out of the court-room, she immediately left her place in the file and stepped into a waiting car, while old Mrs. Gale, Cornelia and Rupert got into another.

2

The funeral took place the next morning.

Riley, as the head of the archæological party, went to the service and the burial to represent them. Roger, though he would have liked to be there to see Dulcie, was glad to be spared. No work was done that morning on the site, so that Roger and Martin were free. Bored with the hotel lounge they went for a run on Roger's Vespa, and sat on a high cliff looking out over the, as it happened, greyish-yellow sea.

After they had talked a little of the inquest, Roger said:

"Did you get any further with Cornelia?"

Martin looked surprised.

"You know what I mean," said Roger.

"I made a pass at her," admitted Martin. "But she said, 'Go away, you silly little man.' I know I'm not very good at these things."

Roger said. "I shouldn't take it that way. I got the impression that Cornelia was a bit of a lemon. Pretty girl, but sharp. Well, it doesn't matter now. She's freed of her papa without your help, and as you didn't take to her——"

"*I* like them cushy," said Martin. "I wonder what'll happen to her. I suppose she'll marry that old Professor. Or will she?"

"I shouldn't think so," said Roger. "She can look around her a bit more easily now. Though, of course, if she marries the old boy, it'll save her trouble: she can go on living at home. I understand that Augustus left the house and contents to his mother in trust for Bose."

"You should be wondering," said Martin with unexpected perspicacity, "what will happen to Dulcibella and her kids. Or just to her. *She's* the stranger in their midst now."

"I want to go and see her," said Roger anxiously, "but I thought I'd better leave it for a day or so."

"You're right," said Martin, giving him a queer look. "Be careful."

3

Roger went along to Geffrye House two days after the funeral. He dismounted from his Vespa outside the front gate, forgetting that there was no longer anyone to prohibit him from driving up to the house. But when he pushed the machine towards the lodge he saw that the lodge was no longer occupied. The curtains were drawn and the front door was closed. He could get no answer.

After pulling repeatedly on an iron handle and hearing a bell ring hollowly within the little house he was going to leave the Vespa there and walk when he became aware that he was being watched. He looked up to see Cornelia. She wore a white dress with a black sash, and in her hand she carried a huge black hat. She was smiling at him mockingly.

"You can ride your horrid little machine up the drive if you like—now," she said. "But I'd much rather you left it there and walked back with *me*." She swung her hat at him in a girlish way.

"All right," said Roger, not very graciously. As they walked along he noticed tyre-marks on the hitherto virgin yellow gravel of the drive. He pulled the Vespa up on to its stand and joined her. When they had walked part of the way without speaking, Cornelia said:

"You're not very communicative."

"I never am."

"And you came to see—Dulcie, not me."

Roger's silence meant "yes". He was beginning to feel uncomfortable as they approached the house, wondering how many people were watching him from behind the blinds, which were still drawn.

"You won't be able to," said Cornelia.

"Why not? Isn't she there?" He tried to keep his tone casual in order not to feed the fire of her obvious triumph, but he could not, any more than he could control the beating of his heart.

"She has gone to London," said Cornelia. "Augustus has made a mess of his will—hasn't made what's called 'proper provision' for his dependants. Dulcie has gone to see his lawyers: it appears they can make application or something, for her and the children. The same applies to me, they tell me, as an unmarried daughter. But I shan't bother."

"Why not? You should. Oh, but of course, I forgot: you're engaged to be married to Professor Bose."

She rounded on him furiously:

"I am not."

"You're not going through with it?"

"Of course not. It was Daddy's idea entirely. Professor Bose doesn't want *me*. He's got what he wants: the Joan Farmer collection and the house, or rather he *will* have when Grandma dies. I'd be merely a liability."

"Yet you stay here. Have you—other plans in mind?"

"Of course."

"Do they concern, in any way, my good friend Martin Praa?"

Somehow, Roger didn't know how, Cornelia had directed their course away from the main drive along a path which led towards the shrubbery. They were now out of sight of the house. Cornelia turned to him with a laugh:

"That silly little man? I'd rather the Professor! I knew all about your plans for me from the start—and Dulcie's. But I'm not so easy to please. Your friend is young; he is also fat and stupid. Oh, he may have brains at his own job; but he's hopelessly slow otherwise."

"He's a very good sort."

"Maybe. But I don't want to marry your 'very good sort'. I like *you*." And to Roger's horror she flung away the black hat and threw her arms round his neck and kissed him on the lips. "You're slow too, darling Roger: but it's an enchanting slowness, the sort that makes me love you, not the slowness of your fat, puffy little friend there." She kissed him again.

He unwound her arms from round his neck. As he did so, he looked up. They had emerged from the shrubbery and were near the boundary wall where it crossed over the mosaic pavement. On the other side the men were working. He saw, disappearing, the head of one of the party. It was not Riley, but that was all he was sure of: the hair was not red.

"Listen, Cornelia," he said in anguish and exasperation.

"Oh yes, I know," said Cornelia, giving him one of her fierce, blue-eyed looks, "you're crazy about Dulcibella. Don't be a fool: let her go. She won't come back."

"Why do you say that?"

"She told me that when she'd seen the lawyers she was going on a cruise: her nerves were in tatters."

"Didn't she give you any message for me?"

"Of course she didn't."

Roger failed to believe her. He thought Cornelia sounded insincere; and he accounted for not having had a letter from Dulcibella by her having entrusted a verbal message to Cornelia. Cornelia went on sulkily:

"She wouldn't trust me. And she's right: if she *had* given me a message for you, I wouldn't have passed it on. Why should I?" She went and picked up the black hat.

They moved on again, past the Joan Farmer hillock and the opened pit, towards the house. Roger would have left her at the porch, but he heard himself hailed from within. As he walked up the steps, Cornelia said to him in an undertone:

"You are a prig and I hate you."

4

Sitting on a stone seat in the porch were Riley and Professor Bose.

"Come here, Royden," called Riley, "we need you for our deliberations. That is, if the Professor agrees."

"Certainly," said Professor Bose, "though I reserve myself the right to co-opt another member—one on my side." He glanced at Cornelia but she swept past him without greeting. "Poor girl!" said Bose. "This business has quite upset her. However, she'll settle down in due course. It's obvious that her place is here, especially now that young Mrs. Gale has left. The house needs a mistress, or it will do when old Mrs. Gale dies." He stopped, seeing Miss Smith in the doorway. "Miss Smith, could you join us? Perhaps you may be wanted to take notes." Miss Smith sat down; she had her notebook and pencil at the ready. "Miss Smith has provisionally accepted the position of *my* secretary," said Bose. "The correspondence at present is enormous; and there will be much to do. Mrs. Gale and I—Mrs. Gale senior, I mean—have decided to admit visitors to this house for payment, on certain days of the week and on public holidays. There will be an extra charge to visit the museum. I am hoping that we may derive a small income towards the upkeep of the place—and I shall negotiate with the National Trust for a salary for one of us as—caretaker."

Riley said: "You've got it all taped, Professor."

"I have thought it my duty to try to preserve what Augustus Gale valued so highly. Unfortunately he was not very practical: he was a visionary."

"What," said Riley, eyeing him keenly, "is your attitude to our work?"

Professor Bose looked enquiring.

"I mean, with regard to the mosaic."

"I have no authority in the matter. The decision rests with Gale's mother."

"Yes—but you could influence her."

"I *could*," said Professor Bose, looking down at his thin hands intertwined on his bony knees.

"Would you?"

"I *might*."

"You mean, for a consideration?"

"That depends."

"On what? On the amount offered?"

"On what is asked for what amount, naturally."

"I see. We should want the right to excavate the mosaic pavement lying within your grounds: to do whatever should seem necessary to us in order to expose the pavement, make records, and so on."

"Oh, I couldn't support that! That's much too general."

"What is your objection?"

"Well, you might, in pursuit of your objective, want to destroy what it is our business to preserve."

"You mean the Joan Farmer hillock?"

"Yes. I am proposing—with Mrs. Gale's concurrence—to rail off the hillock and make it the highlight of our tour of the house and grounds. I should be here to conduct parties round and explain the features, with the aid of diagrams and reconstructions."

"How Joan Farmer would have opened her eyes! But if we make a neat job of the mosaic without destroying your hillock, don't you think it would be an added attraction?"

"It might." Professor Bose pulled at his beard. "We could keep the mosaic covered and charge extra. We could, I suppose, erect a wooden structure over it for protection. But these things cost money."

"You could recoup your expenditure from entrance fees."

"Over a long period. Where is the capital to come from?"

"I don't know," said Riley, suddenly angry with the obstructive, greedy old man. "Not from *me*, that's sure." He rose. "I'm just an underpaid archæologist."

"Then I can't help you."

"What will you do with the mosaic? Gale's part of it, I mean: we shall carry on as before."

"It will have to be filled in."

"You'll ruin it. A good deal of damage has been done already."

"I am bound to try to preserve what Augustus valued."

"No, you're not, sir. Augustus was crazy about this Joan Farmer woman, which excuses him. But you're not crazy about anything. You're thinking about profit. You want a bribe. You won't get it, not through us."

The Professor rose, trembling with rage.

"Get out!"

"When I'm ready," said Riley, walking up the steps and in through the open door. "But first of all I have something to do."

He strolled into the deserted drawing-room, where the furniture was now covered in dust-sheets. He switched on the lights. The great crystal chandelier looked even more incongruous in the morning than in the afternoon. Riley strolled to a small table and found there what he sought: a wooden tray, on which were displayed small cubes of marble, black, white and rusty red; through some of them holes had been drilled, just as Martin and Roger had told him: he had not had time or opportunity to do more than glance at them before. He shovelled the whole trayful of cubes into his jacket pocket as Professor Bose, catching up with him, entered the room.

"What are you doing? Stop thief!" squeaked Bose.

Riley laughed. "Rescuing Clio from the vandals."

Cornelia had come and was standing behind him. Bose turned.

"Cornelia, call the police!"

Cornelia said coolly:

"You old donkey, have you forgotten there's no telephone?"

"Cornelia! Go out at once and get help. I mean to be obeyed."

"Go to hell!" said Cornelia. "You've got no hold over me any more. You don't really think I'm going to marry you now that Daddy's dead? Go and marry Joan Farmer —or Grandma."

Riley laughed.

Cornelia gave him a savage look.

"You clear out," she said furiously. "I hate you and your beastly mosaic."

"Really? What a girl!" said Riley, rattling the cubes in his pocket.

"Put those back: they're not yours," said Cornelia.

Riley laughed again.

Cornelia ran out of the room. Riley strode past the Professor, pushing him aside, and left the house without a backward look, not hurrying at all, running the marble cubes through the fingers of his left hand which was in his jacket pocket. He ran the other hand through his red hair.

"Whew!" he said to himself. "Now I've messed up everything."

Roger and Miss Smith had been left in the porch together, events having happened too quickly for them to be able to take part. Miss Smith went indoors to soothe the Professor. Roger followed Riley.

5

When Fitzbrown walked into the Superintendent's office that afternoon, Mallett said:

"An awkward situation has arisen. I've just had a phone call from Geffrye House."

"I thought they weren't on the phone."

"They're not," said Mallet. "They sent their man Brook to phone from the nearest call-box, on the main road half a mile away. They say they were robbed this morning."

"They can hardly expect *you* to do anything about it if they are so slow in getting the message through."

"Ah, but they lay a definite charge against someone." He leaned across the desk. "It's a strange story. I shall have to go straight there and investigate. Nuisance: I'm busy. Thought I'd heard the last of those crazy people for a bit."

"Tell me the gist of it," said Fitzbrown.

"They—or rather this old Professor Bose who's in charge there at present—accuse the head of the archæological expedition, the tall, red-haired fellow called Riley, of having pinched some Roman mosaics."

"Roman mosaics? How could he? They're in the ground."

"I don't know. That's why I'm going out there myself to find out the facts. Care to come with me?"

Fitzbrown looked at his watch.

"Sure. Especially as I've got something I want to discuss with you."

"About what?"

"About the death of Augustus Gale."

6

"What's on your mind?" said Mallett as they were driving along the main road.

"That verdict."

"You don't agree with it? Surely it is obvious."

"It may be correct," said Fitzbrown, "but it was reached by a series of *non sequiturs*. I stayed on to hear the rest of the evidence because I couldn't believe my ears. I knew what would happen, and it did. It was a masterpiece of illogicality: bridging the gaps with a surmise which no one seemed to notice."

"But—"

"Yes, I know: Gale took a dose of mercury in some form. The mercury tablet got into his tea from Royden's case. Therefore, it was assumed, Gale got the tablet and put it into his own tea."

"But—"

"Wait a minute: *why* was this assumption made? Because Gale was known to be a very strange man, an eccentric. His way of life was odd, and he enforced it on other people."

"He was also proved to have been a very irascible, excitable man. There was other evidence of that, by the way, as well as what was heard in court. The archæologists said he struck his *wife* as well as his son, in front of them. We kept that out. It wasn't necessary as there was plenty of other evidence of his lack of control: the episode of the port wine, for instance. *I* thought the man was as mad as a hatter, I must confess: he was an exhibitionist."

"Perhaps he was," said Fitzbrown quietly. "But you have no proof that he committed suicide. Did you examine Royden's case and the bottle for fingerprints?"

"We did. There were no fingerprints other than those of Royden himself."

"None of Augustus Gale's?"

"No."

"Didn't that surprise you?"

"Perhaps he was wearing gloves," said Mallett. "The ladies were, and he was in fancy dress."

"Gloves on a man who was in the middle of dining? Hardly. There were no gloves on the cadaver. We established, didn't we, just when he got the tablet—*if* he got it."

"Gale must have got the tablet," agreed Mallett, "from Royden's case, which was in Royden's room, between the end of dinner and the beginning of this tea-drinking. That is, between about half-past six and seven. We learnt that from the old lady. As also the motive, namely, that his wife was planning to run off with another man. We kept that, too, out of the inquest. I told the Coroner about it, but he agreed it had better be kept out for every reason. For one thing we have only the old lady's word for it, and she's so obviously hostile to Gale's second wife."

"Quite so," said Fitzbrown. "But my point is, we have to assume that Gale knew where to go for the tablet or tablets—"

"Not a very great assumption. Royden admitted he had displayed the case to the women—and you know how women talk."

"I think it unlikely," said Fitzbrown quietly, "that Gale's wife or daughter would have noticed and reported to Gale that among the bottles in one of Royden's cases there was one which contained biniodide of mercury. It's not an easy name to remember, especially if you've never heard it before."

"No," said Mallett, "maybe not. But the bottle was plainly labelled 'Poison'. One of the ladies could easily have remarked on *that* to Gale."

"Not impossible, though unlikely."

"As I see it," Mallett pressed home his advantage, "old Mrs. Gale told her son about his wife; in a fit of rage he went to Royden's room, opened the case, saw the bottle labelled poison and decided to do away with himself—"

"I know," interrupted Fitzbrown. "Perhaps that's what did happen. All I say is, it's an assumption."

"Have you got a better explanation?"

"No. But if conjecture is in order, there are one or two things that occur to me about this affair which *could* be explained differently."

"For instance?"

"Have you noticed in how many people's interest it was to get rid of Augustus Gale?"

"Go on."

"Apart from his wife and this young fellow Royden who owns the tablets—"

"That's a big 'apart' if they were planning to run off together."

"I know. I don't except them entirely: I merely want to exclude them for the moment. I'll come back to them afterwards. But there were others who might have wanted to get rid of Gale: those who benefit under the will—"

"You surely don't suspect old Mrs. Gale of murdering her son?"

"No, I don't. If I'm any judge of human nature," said Fitzbrown, "she really was devoted to her son—though in my line, and in yours, one never takes even maternal love for granted, nor any other kind, no matter how close the tie."

"No indeed."

But old Mrs. Gale is *too* old. She's over eighty. She had a very comfortable home while her son lived. Why should she want to get rid of him? All she acquires is a lot of trouble, loss from death duties and a reduced income, apart from the worry of it all. No, but the old Professor gets a home, and when Mrs. Gale dies, a house. *He* stands to gain."

"That proves nothing."

"I know. I am simply pointing out motives. If I could *prove* something, I wouldn't waste time analysing these people's characters. There are also Augustus's children: the grown-up ones, I mean. He was on bad terms with his son. Rupert Gale said that Augustus ordered him out of the house, and it's clear that they had a violent quarrel, before many witnesses, that very morning. Then there's the daughter, Cornelia, who was being forced into a marriage with that old Professor-codger. She could hardly have been going into *that* of her own free will, a pretty girl like that."

"She could have cleared out," growled Mallett.

"Perhaps. Perhaps she was under Daddy's domination. It can happen. I've known cases—"

"So have I."

"We could try to find out," said Fitzbrown, "when we arrive."

"We could. Then," said Mallett, "there are those three young men."

"The archæologists? Yes. There's Royden, who owned the poison and is in love with Augustus Gale's wife, now widow. There's young Praa, who looks harmless enough, but as you would say, you never know. As for the redheaded Irishman, he looks fierce."

"He does so."

"He seems a charming fellow," said Fitzbrown. "My only point is the rather theoretical one that Gale was very much in the way of the archæological expedition. He had apparently refused to let them explore the piece of mosaic pavement which lies on *his* side of the wall; and—"

"But they have a big piece on their own side!" protested Mallett. "Surely that'd be enough for them! It was more than enough for me when I went along to look at it yesterday. Have you seen it?"

"I have," said Fitzbrown. "A bunch of fat women wearing brassières and bathing trunks: Riley's words, not mine. He doesn't like the mosaics, or so he says, and he thinks it's typical of the Romans to depict coarse women of their own day and call them Muses. But, you see, that's irrelevant. The fact is that archæological discoveries mean fame, publicity and a great deal of money nowadays to those engaged on them; and for these young men Augustus Gale was a serious obstacle to their plans. Also, Riley told me that Augustus was going to destroy the piece on his side: he had already begun removing *tesserae*, for some quite frivolous purpose, apparently out of sheer perversity—or was it a queer ramification of his devotion to Joan Farmer? Was he afraid lest the Nine Muses and their mother might rival his beloved Joan in public interest! Was it—"

"Wait a minute!" exclaimed Mallett. "Did you say *tesserae?*"

"I did."

"Those are the small cubes out of which a mosaic picture is built up?"

"They are."

"That's what the call was about!"

"What call?" said Fitzbrown, who had forgotten for what purpose they were now driving along to Geffrye House.

"The robbery! The Professor accuses this fellow Riley of having lifted a pocketful of *tesserae* from the drawing-room! *Tesserae!* I wondered what exactly they were, but I didn't ask him. He was so excited—and, anyhow, these professors talk so much. He'd have wanted to tell me a whole long history. I hadn't time to listen to a lecture. *Tesserae*: that was it."

"*Tesserae* is the Greek for 'four'. They're cubes, you see, with square faces—four-sided. Get it?"

"Don't *you* start," said Mallett. "Here we are."

They turned in through the gates which now stood open, and drew up before the front porch.

Professor Bose was standing on the steps. Close behind him was Miss Smith, notebook and pencil in hand, and behind her, in the shadows of the vestibule, was Cornelia.

7

Roger, Martin and Riley were sitting in the lounge of the hotel. Riley had just thrown on to the round table in front of them the handful of *tesserae* from his pocket.

"Where did you get them?" gasped Martin.

"I swiped them."

"You did?"

"I walked right in and took them off the drawing-room table when I realised the old goat was going to be as un-co-operative as Gale."

"Couldn't you have talked him round?" said Roger.

"Never—not that old fool. We might, in time, have got round Gale because he was sincere in his resistance. I mean, he was fighting to defend something he loved—or someone, if you like—and if we could have persuaded him that there was no menace to Joan Farmer, or as I was planning to do, that *our* activities would bring thousands of fresh admirers to Joan Farmer's feet, so to speak, he would have given way I would have painted him a picture of Joan Farmer sitting on her hillock like a queen on her throne, while those who came to admire those fat Muses would have remained to dote on Joan."

"They wouldn't have," said Roger. "There was nothing to see on the hillock. People nowadays won't admire what they can't see. That would require imagination."

"Yes," said Riley, "but I was going to suggest to Gale —at the right moment, you understand, when the preliminary softening-up process was finished—I was going to suggest that he should rail off the hillock and put on the top a tasteful monument of some kind: a replica of Joan Farmer's summer-house, for instance; perhaps even a marble statue of herself sitting, pen in hand, looking soulful or thoughtful, holding an open book with a quote from one of her own plays."

"Horrible!" said Roger.

"Not at all. I know just the man who could do it," said Riley. "He's done a beauty of a woman sitting on a mound outside— well, never mind where; but that marble woman has often nearly brought me to my knees, and has certainly brought a lump to my throat. I could have convinced Gale that it was a good idea and then he would have let us have our mosaic. I'm sorry Gale was cut off, God rest his soul. I liked the man in spite of everything."

"So did I," said Martin heartily and unconvincingly. Roger remained silent: from him such a tribute would have been hypocritical.

Riley began fitting together the *tesserae* into their original pattern.

"They come from the left thigh of Clio," he said, "with a bit of the bikini, if that's what it's called nowadays. See?"

"I remember the bit that was missing," said Martin. "I have my sketch. You're right. But what are you going to do with these?"

"Keep them."

"But they're stolen, however you look at it."

"In a way," said Riley. "In another way not. You see, they really are the property of the nation. Nobody has a right to destroy objects of national interest. And you Britishers are so lacking in modern culture that—"

Roger and Martin groaned: they had heard all this and knew it by heart.

"That you have to preserve," continued Riley calmly, "all the bits of culture you can find from the past—most of them, incidentally, the work of invaders. Now if you could have another invasion—"

"We have," said Roger, "from Eire. I forget how many every year."

Riley fitted in the last *tesserae*: on the table was a triangle of flesh and the edge of the garment he had called a bikini.

"What's your plan?" said Roger.

"I thought one of us could take these up to London and show them to someone in authority. Perhaps we'd better get hold of someone weighty from the Society of Roman Studies, or Burlington House, or the British Museum, or what-have-you. Then the next step would be to approach the Ministry of Works, I suppose. It'll take time. In Eire we'd do it more sensibly. The three of us would just go tonight with bags and spades and lift the rest of the pavement before old Bose destroys it. But I don't think he'll do any more harm because of its money value. The question now is, which of us is to go to London. I can't leave the work. Besides, I'd like to be here in case Bose makes trouble. Will you toss up? Settle it between yourselves. I don't mind." He got up and strolled off: "I'm going back to the dig. See you at lunchtime."

8

Roger leaned forward eagerly.

"Martin, do you mind if I go?"

Martin looked awkward. "No, I don't mind, Roger. But I think it would be better if I went, or rather if you didn't."

"Why? I was going to ask Riley to give me a week's leave in any case. I happen to want to go up to London."

"Exactly."

"What do you mean, 'exactly'?"

"I mean, it's what one would expect you to do. Roger, don't get mad at me, but I don't think you should go—not yet, anyway."

"Why not?" blustered Roger.

"You'd be going after Mrs. Gale, wouldn't you?"

"That's my business. Is there any reason—now—why I shouldn't see Mrs. Gale if I wish and she doesn't object?"

"Roger, you're a fool."

"I don't see—"

"No. That's what makes you a fool— Oh, thank God, it's only twenty past." He went across to the bar and came back carrying two beers. "Roger, I wanted to say this to you," he said, "but I haven't known how to begin. Cheers." He drank. "Roger, there are some damned unpleasant rumours going about."

"Rumours?"

"Gossip. Talk. Do you know— No, of course you don't—" He would have liked to say, "Love is blind," but didn't dare. "In spite of the verdict, people are talking. They are saying that it's funny that the poison should have got into Gale's tea while we were in the house."

"Who are 'people'?" said Roger.

"The gossip has several strata. The local inhabitants regard us as foreigners: that's nothing new. They don't like us, simply because we're strangers."

"They like our money."

"They're not the dangerous ones except that they provide the climate for gossip. They dislike the expedition as such, and they aren't thinking out a case against us. They know—the workmen and presumably therefore their families know—that we were held up because of Gale's opposition. Therefore, they say, we bumped him off."

"What rot!"

"That sort of gossip will die down naturally, because it's fantasy without support, without nourishment. But inside that there is a more dangerous kind."

"Dangerous to whom?"

"To all of us, and especially to—you."

"Me?"

"Some people say more specifically, 'Funny the poison-tablet came out of that young archæologist's kit. Why did he bring it with him? He must have had a reason for carrying the poison around.'"

"I explained that when I gave my evidence."

"Your explanation sounds as weak as the truth often does, Roger, to people who want to believe ill of you. Some of our own chaps have said in my hearing that you were an ass to carry poison around with you. As for the idea of your needing a first-aid case, they laugh. They say, what first-aider ever needed instruments?"

"I built up the contents of that case on other expeditions—abroad."

"Yes, but you don't need them here. You can get a doctor or a dentist. And, anyhow, those with any knowledge are saying nobody uses biniodide of mercury nowadays: nurses in hospital just boil instruments. You know Crowley's father is a doctor and he says—"

"Look here, Martin, are you trying to tell me that members of our own party think I poisoned Gale?"

"They haven't said as much as that; they've been joking about it, saying it would have been a useful thing to do to get Gale out of the way, and you'd deserve public recognition if you did it. That's not the same as saying you did it. But it intensifies what I call the climate of opinion in which suspicion grows."

"*Whose* suspicion?"

"I don't know. But if such talk gets round to the police, they may feel obliged to do something about it. They're sensitive to criticism these days, like everybody else."

Roger laughed. "What *can* they do? They'll have to get some evidence before they can arrest me. Gale was poisoned: we know that. We know he was poisoned with biniodide of mercury. We know the tablet came out of my case. But there isn't the slightest reason to suggest that *I* gave it to him. As for proof, I doubt if any proof is possible. What can they do? Exhume Gale? That'll prove no more than we know already—that he died of mercury poisoning."

Martin was shocked. "Roger, for heaven's sake don't talk like that, except to me! Anyone who didn't know you would think it *proved* you did it and were bluffing it off."

"Well," said Roger, unrepentant, "if it's a murder, it's a jolly clever one, isn't it? If anyone gave Gale the tablet, he knew that what you call the 'climate of opinion' was just right. But I don't believe it: I believe Gale took it himself."

"So do I," said Martin. "But remember this: though, as you say, no one can *prove* anything *now*, they can, if they *suspect* you, make things very uncomfortable."

Martin's face was not the right shape for the expression of strong feeling, admonition, anxiety, nor anything penetrating or unpleasant. Nevertheless he could look serious; and seriousness so little suited him that Roger's attention was arrested.

"Martin, what are you trying to tell me? Out with it! I can see this is all leading up to something you don't like to say."

"Just this, Roger: let *me* take those *tesserae* to London instead of you."

"Why?"

"Because—you very much want to go."

"Yes."

"Because you want to see Mrs. Gale?"

"Yes. But what the hell business is that of anybody's?"

"Roger, in the present 'climate of opinion', your chasing after Mrs. Gale will be to some people a *proof* that you bumped off her husband. It's the commonest motive for murder, you know."

"Except money."

"I wouldn't know: neck and neck as motives, I'd have said. Anyhow, the people who are talking will have what they want against you—motive."

"Why should I care," said Roger, "what these half-baked provincials say about me?"

"Roger, I've told you, it's not only local gossip you have to consider, it's going to spread further. It *has* spread further. You will be seriously affected in your career. This thing will follow you everywhere, especially if you marry Mrs. Gale. You'll never get rid of the aftereffects. It's not funny, you know, to be turned down when you deserve a job because some busybody looks up your past or your private life, or some enemy passes on the rumour."

"I don't care."

"You don't now, but you will."

"Martin, it's not like you to talk in this old-man wiseacre way."

"You're my friend. Roger, all I ask is, stay here and let *me* take the *tesserae* to London."

They both looked down at the scrap of flesh represented by the mosaic *tesserae*, which Riley had arranged on the table. There was silence for a while, then Roger swept the pieces off the table and put them in his jacket pocket.

"Sorry, Martin, but I must go." When they reached the bar, Roger said: "I suppose this makes *me* the receiver of stolen goods."

"That's another thing that worries me. I don't think Riley ought to have left the baby on *your* doorstep, or mine."

"Don't worry," said Roger. "I've thought of that, too. I'm not quite such a fool as you think."

VII

Superintendent Mallett and Dr. Fitzbrown, on their arrival at Geffrye House, were shown into the drawing-room by Robert Brook, wearing a black alpaca coat. They looked round with interest. The blinds and curtains were still drawn and Robert had switched on the chandelier. As Robert was leaving the room Mallett stopped him.

"You were satisfied with the verdict?"

Brook looked aggressive. "I don't know what you mean. It was no affair of mine. What the Coroner said went for me as well as the family." He shook his head. "We do miss the old man here: I mean Mr. Gale."

"I thought you said Mr. Gale was hard to work for. In court you made out he was always having attacks of violent temper."

"So he was, but none of us took any notice. It was part of the place, see? Made it more lively like. If Mr. Gale hadn't lost his temper now and then and stirred things up, it would have been pretty dull."

"Then you don't really think he was insane?"

"Not he. Even the Coroner couldn't say that. 'Balance of the mind disturbed,' says the Coroner. You couldn't call that insanity." He grinned. "The balance of *my* mind is disturbed most days by something or other."

"Thank you, Brook," said Mallett, dismissing him as he heard a step outside. Professor Bose entered.

"Ah, Inspector—Superintendent—and Doctor. I'm glad you've come. This is a shocking business."

"Please describe exactly what happened," said Mallett.

Professor Bose invited them to sit down. They sat uncomfortably on uncomfortable eighteenth-century chairs. The Professor described how Riley, after a conversation about the future of the mosaic pavement, had lost his temper, marched into the house, snatched the *tesserae* off the round table—"There!"—he pointed with bony finger—and having put them into his pocket, had gone off.

"When did this happen?"

"This morning."

"Why didn't you let us know at once?"

Professor Bose looked down. "There was a dispute as to who should go. As you are aware, there is no telephone in this house. In the end I sent the servant—Robert Brook —to the telephone call-box on the main road. Anyway, Superintendent, the time element hardly matters here. We have a clear case of robbery performed under our eyes. The *tesserae* were the property of the late Mr. Gale, and they are therefore now the property of his legal heir, his mother, Mrs. Gale. They must be recovered and the thief must be punished."

"Were there any other witnesses of this incident?"

"Yes. Miss Cornelia Gale was there, and so was Miss Smith, my secretary. One of the other archæologists was there: the young man who has caused the present tragedy by so carelessly carrying poison about in an unlocked case."

"Royden?" said Dr. Fitzbrown.

"I believe that *is* his name."

Cornelia had entered a moment before.

"Of course that's his name: Roger Royden, the man who killed my father."

They all turned to look at her.

"Don't say that, my dear," admonished the Professor. "That is slander." He smiled a small, academic smile to announce a small, academic joke: "Superintendent Mallett will take down what you say and use it *against* you."

Mallett opened his mouth to protest, but the Professor was continuing:

"Gentlemen, you know my fiancée, Miss Cornelia Gale."

"I'm not your fiancée," stormed Cornelia. "I never was, and you know it. I hate you, because you encouraged my father in all this Joan Farmer nonsense. You know you did: making him buy rubbish for that beastly museum and talking to him for hours about the past. If he was mad, it was partly your fault—*largely* your fault. I hate you. And I hate Roger Royden because he killed my father."

She still spoke angrily, but not so violently as before. She sat down. Mallett and Fitzbrown reseated themselves.

"Do you think it's fair," said Mallett, "to throw out such an accusation without proof!"

"Proof!" said Cornelia. "What more proof do you want? He brought the poison into the house, didn't he? And he had the only real motive for getting rid of Daddy."

"You mean," said Mallett, pretending to misunderstand, "he was the one deputed to get rid of your father because your father wouldn't let the archaeologists work at the mosaic?"

"Don't be idiotic," said Cornelia. "As if they cared about the stupid mosaic! Riley has told everybody it's of no artistic value. He could easily have talked Daddy round, anyway, with that blarney of his; Daddy stormed a lot but he could be got round. No: I mean Roger Royden was in love with my stepmother. Let him deny it if he can. You knew it all along, but the police were bribed to shut up. Weren't they?"

She had not noticed that the door behind her was being held open.

"Mr. Royden, sir," said Robert.

Roger walked in.

2

"Perhaps I'm mistaken," he said. "But I think I heard my name mentioned." He bowed ironically towards Cornelia.

"You did," said Cornelia. She was about to begin again on her tirade when Mallett interrupted.

"Just a minute. We seem to be being diverted from the business which brought us here. Shall we settle that first? Then, perhaps, if Miss Gale still wishes, we can take her statement. At present I should like to hear her evidence on the alleged theft of these *tesserae*. Mr. Royden, we are here in response to a call from Professor Bose, who says that your colleague, Mr. Riley, took some objects called *tesserae*, part of a Roman mosaic pavement inside the grounds of this house; took them from this table here against the will of the owner, who is of course the late Augustus Gale's heir. The beneficiaries also are interested, naturally. Perhaps you would prefer to withdraw while we go into this matter, unless you have anything to add?"

"I've got plenty to add," said Roger. He pulled the *tesserae* out of his jacket pocket and threw them on to the round table from which they had been taken. "Here you are. Here's you're stolen property."

The marble cubes rattled down on to the highly polished surface of the table.

3

Martin Praa strolled on to the site, where Riley had arrived an hour or so before. He went up to Riley.

"Look here, can I have a word with you?"

Riley looked at his watch.

"Break for tea!" he called out to the others.

He and Martin went and sat on a log.

"It's about Roger," began Martin.

"He's the one who's going to London? I thought so," said Riley. "How did you decide?"

"He wants to go."

"Of course."

"Why," said Martin accusingly, "didn't you say I was to go?"

"Because I knew he'd go, anyway, and I thought it would be best if he had some sort of excuse."

"You knew he'd go?"

"Of course," said Riley.

"After Gale's wife?"

"Gale's widow," corrected Riley. "That's different, surely."

"Riley, you know what people are saying about Roger?"

"Naturally I know: it's my business to know what's being said in so far as it concerns us; unfortunately, because I'm not paid extra for it."

"And you think it's all right for him to go chasing off to London less than a week after Gale's death?"

"Pursuing the beautiful widow, you mean? I can't see why not. People can talk as much as they like but they can't *prove* anything. That's the beauty of poison."

"Riley, it'll ruin Roger's career."

"Maybe," said Riley, "he thinks it's worth it. It's not much of a career to ruin, now, is it?" He leaned down and drew out a bottle from among the long, cool ferns under the log. "Have some beer." They drank.

Martin shifted his ground. "Do you think he'll bother about the *tesserae* once he's there?"

Riley considered. "That's another matter. I have wondered about that. Also, I didn't like making him a sort of receiver of stolen goods. Your law over here is as mutton-headed now as it was in the past: it'll make no distinction between Royden and a common fence, I suppose."

"None," said Martin, with added reproach in his tone. They drank again.

"Another thing worries me," said Riley.

"What now?"

"Will he go to London at all?"

"What makes you say that?" Martin asked eagerly. "I had the same idea when he left me."

"Why?"

"Well," said Martin, "he picked up the *tesserae* after saying he had to go to London, and then I saw him go past the window, in the direction— Well, I got the feeling he wasn't going to the station. He may just have been going for a walk, but if so it was in the direction of Geffrye House. I watched him out of sight and he was heading this way. I assumed he was coming to the site here, perhaps to have another word with you. He didn't come here?"

"No. He hasn't been here."

"Then he must have gone to the house."

"Why should he do that?" said Riley.

"I don't know. I thought perhaps you'd know."

Riley thought. "I see you haven't heard the latest rumour."

"I've heard plenty," said Martin. "Don't tell me there's more."

"There is, and how!" He pulled out another bottle and filled Martin's glass and his own. "The latest story is, it's not the beautiful Widow Gale—fair Dulcibella—he's after, but Cornelia."

"Good God!" said Martin mildly. "Any evidence? Or is it the usual guesswork? I didn't know our chaps were such gossips. Tell me more."

"Crowley over there," said Riley, nodding in the direction of one of the party, "is no friend of Roger's, as you know."

"I know. They loathe each other. Crowley's jealous of Roger."

"Crowley's observations, therefore, may be biased. But I don't think so. Crowley has reported something to Roger's advantage."

"Really?"

"Crowley says he saw Roger kissing Cornelia Gale in the garden this morning. He happened, so he says, to look over the wall at that moment and saw them locked in an embrace. Now if Roger will only marry Cornelia instead of Dulcibella, his reputation will be cleared."

"You mean, he'll no longer be suspected of poisoning Gale?"

"Roughly that."

Martin swore. Then he said: "Riley, I don't believe Roger has changed his tack. I mean, I don't believe he's after Cornelia. I think he's still after Mrs. Gale."

"Do you think Crowley made up the story of his kissing Cornelia? Crowley hasn't much imagination, you know, and what he has, he wouldn't waste rehabilitating Roger."

"No, I don't think he made it up."

"Then you think Roger was just philandering with Cornelia, in the absence of Dulcibella?"

"No, I don't think that either. Roger's no philanderer. You know that."

Riley laughed. Martin just smiled.

"Do you know what I think?" said Martin.

"Not always," said Riley.

"I think Cornelia kissed Roger. I think she's keen on him."

"Poor girl. He gets all the luck."

Martin went on solemnly:

"Roger wouldn't have made up to Cornelia because he asked *me* to."

"What?"

"He did it to please Mrs. Gale. He said she wanted him to find a husband or something for Cornelia, because Cornelia was repressed by Augustus and couldn't get around."

"And you accepted the assignment?" said Riley with a queer look.

"I agreed to go along and look her over. But she had no use for me. She had no eyes for anyone but Roger. Didn't you notice? She was always getting him into corners. I'm certain from what he said just now that he's just as keen as ever on Mrs. Gale."

"But you say he didn't go to the station. If he was determined to go to London he could have caught the connection at four o'clock and been in London by six-thirty. But you say he came this way. Doesn't that look as if he had switched from Dulcie to Cornelia?"

"I don't know. I don't think so," said Martin, "from what he said."

"Has he got the *tesserae*? He's missed the only train to London this evening. Damn! Why didn't I go myself?"

"Yes. I wondered that," said Martin unkindly.

"I thought I ought to stick around here and keep things under control. But I'd have done better to go, or send you. Roger's unreliable in his present state of mind. But as I told you, I had his interest at heart. I thought it'd give him an excuse for going to London. I was sure he was going to ask me for leave of absence, and that'd make people talk more than ever. So if I sent him, they'd have to shut up. But if I'd known he wouldn't go this evening—"

"It doesn't matter," said Martin. "There'll be no one there he wants to see, anyway—not on Saturday. Nothing can be done till Monday about the *tesserae.*"

"Damn! I forgot that. Though how anyone who's ever been in London on a Saturday can forget it, God knows. But he mustn't have those *tesserae* over the weekend. He might lose them, and also they're my responsibility. *I* swiped them. I must get them back." He got up. "Where is he? At the hotel? Oh no, you said he went out." A look of concern began to dawn. "You said he came *this* way. Yet he hasn't been here. You don't think he's gone to the house? If so, what for? My God, you don't think he's fool enough to be scared by the police!"

Riley set off.

Martin subsided on to the log, finished the beer, and followed Riley round the outside of the boundary wall towards the entrance. He thought morosely that he was always following somebody with the best of intentions, and getting no thanks for it.

4

Superintendent Mallett looked from the *tesserae* on the table to Roger's red, furious face, and from him to the pale but no less furious face of Professor Bose. He ignored Cornelia.

"Are those the stolen goods in question, Professor?" he said.

Professor Bose got up, went to the table, studied the *tesserae*, turned some of them over. He said:

"They appear to be. But I cannot tell if all have been returned."

"This is the lot," said Roger to Mallett, "I assure you."

Mallett said: "I presume you no longer wish to lay a charge, Professor."

"Certainly I do," said Bose.

"Against whom?"

"Against the man Riley who took the *tesserae* from this table."

"Did you get the *tesserae* from Mr. Riley?" Mallett said to Roger.

"No," said Roger.

"Then where did you get them?"

"I took them myself," said Roger shamelessly.

"Oh," gasped Cornelia, "what a liar you are! I *saw* Riley take them."

"You were mistaken," said Roger with a grin. "You are often mistaken, Miss Gale. You get excited sometimes —hysterical—and you imagine things."

"Mr. Royden says he took these objects," said Mallett, ignoring Cornelia's exclamation of rage. "Professor, do you want to bring a charge against him?"

"Of course not," said Professor Bose irritably. "It was Riley who took them. This man Royden wasn't there. It's a trick to exculpate Riley."

"I *was* there," said Roger quickly. "I was there, you know. I was sitting in the porch with you when your conversation with Mr. Riley took place. You were too excited to notice, I suppose. Miss Smith was there, too. She has a cooler head: she will remember seeing me there."

The secretary had entered quietly and was standing behind Professor Bose's chair, on which he had reseated himself. She carried her notebook and pencil. She did not glance up as she replied:

"Yes. Mr. Royden was there."

"During the conversation in the porch," said Bose. "But it was Riley who took the *tesserae*, wasn't it, my dear? You remember?"

"I'm afraid I don't—quite," said Miss Smith with a glazed look.

"But Miss Gale saw Riley. You followed him into the drawing-room, and saw him sweep the *tesserae* off the table and put them into his pocket."

Cornelia's blue eyes flashed as she glared at Roger.

"I'm not quite sure if I did. It *may* have been Mr. Royden."

"My dear!" said Professor Bose.

"I'm *not* your dear!" said Cornelia, rounding on him. "I've told you, all that sort of thing is over between us. I don't have to keep up the idiotic farce any longer. To me you are just a horrid old man who made use of my father when he was alive, and who is partly responsible for his death."

She glowered at each of them in turn. She forgot, however, to glower at Miss Smith, and so she missed the small smile that crossed the secretary's lips.

Mallett stood up.

"You don't need me any more. You can't bring a charge on such confused evidence, Professor. You have the stolen objects back. With that you had better be content. I don't think any of this would sound good in a court of law. If any of the *tesserae* are missing, perhaps you'll let me know."

He left. Fitzbrown followed him. On the steps of the porch they passed Riley, but Mallett did not stop. In the drive they passed Martin Praa.

"The gathering of the clan," said Mallett as they drove back. "I say, that young woman is a spitfire. Did what she said tie up in any way with what you were saying on the way out here?"

"Not at all," said Fitzbrown. "Wash it out. They're all cracked, not only poor Gale. I was only speculating on motive. Let's leave it at that."

"Yes," said Mallett. "No purpose can be served by going into the matter further. It's a curious thing, you know, but whenever a man dies you can always find quite a number of people who benefit by his death or have some motive for wanting him out of the way. I never bother about motive until I have some concrete reason for suspecting a particular person. Here we have no concrete reason for suspecting murder at all. Otherwise I would have asked the Coroner to adjourn the inquest. But there seemed no real reason—"

"Quite true. Forget it."

VIII

From that time onward the police took no further interest in the death of Augustus Gale nor in the affairs of the Gale family and their connections. The verdict was accepted by them and by the community, and gossip died away. The tensions among the principal actors, their hates and loves, were resolved among themselves, and never became public. This is what happened.

2

As soon as Mallett's car was heard driving away, Roger picked up a handful of the *tesserae* and said:

"I'm going to London with these. Now go on: ring the police again and get them to arrest me. By the time you get to a call-box, Mallett will have arrived back at the station and he'll be in a towering rage. What are you waiting for?"

"How dare you!" said Bose.

Cornelia remarked: "He's going to London to see Dulcie. It has nothing to do with the *tesserae*. Has it?" She turned to Roger. Roger, deceived by her apparent mildness, said:

"Can you give me Mrs. Gale's London address?"

Cornelia laughed. "He doesn't know her address!"

Roger looked at Miss Smith. "I suppose you know it."

"No."

"But somebody must know it. What about letters?"

"She left orders that no letters were to be forwarded."

At that moment Riley walked in.

"What are you after, Royden?" His eye caught the *tesserae* lying on the table. "What right have you to give them back?"

"I have enough to show people," said Roger, rattling the marble cubes in his pocket. "I don't need to carry a couple of pounds of them round with me."

"Why didn't you catch the four o'clock?"

"If I had gone straight to the station, these people would have had me arrested. They could have, you know. I was a receiver of stolen property."

"If you're afraid, give them to me," said Riley angrily. "If they could have you arrested for carrying a hundred *tesserae*, so they can if you're carrying twenty." He held out his hand.

"They won't have me arrested," said Roger. "I think I've put a spoke in their wheel. The police won't take any notice of any further accusation: Mallett thinks they're all mad. And so they are, if this afternoon's proceedings are anything to go by." He glared at Cornelia. "This young woman here accused me of poisoning her father."

"I didn't."

"You did; not in front of *me*, in front of the Superintendent and the doctor. And why? 'Hell hath no fury—'"

"Oh, shut up!" Cornelia rushed out of the room.

"Not a Regency expression," said Roger.

"Poor girl, she's overwrought," said the Professor.

"Rubbish," said Miss Smith.

The Professor turned right round and adjusted his spectacles to stare at her. Miss Smith spoke to him only.

"You're a great deal too kind and considerate. She insults you to your face, and you say almost nothing. Let her go. You don't know what a spitfire she is. Everybody's afraid of her. Now I've said my say, I'll pack and leave. But I repeat, I think you're a thousand times too good for her."

"My dear young lady," said Professor Bose, "those are the first words of appreciation I've had in this house since Augustus died. Certainly you shall not pack and leave. I can't do without you. Stay and be my—secretary, as we arranged. Let us go and talk about it together. I'm sure we shall be able to come to terms which will suit us both very well indeed."

He rose and with a courtly bow offered her his arm. They went out together.

3

Roger and Riley looked after them. So did Martin, who passed them in the doorway.

"The old goat seems to have gotten himself another bride," said Roger. "Not as good-looking as Cornelia but more useful."

"Imagine that!" said Riley. "I bet he'll make her work."

"And I bet she'll make him pay for it," said Roger. "And she'll give the rest of the household hell—if they stay. Cornelia especially will have something to shout about."

"There'll be murder done," said Martin. "Real murder. Don't leave any of those poison tablets behind, Roger."

"The police still have them."

"Cornelia can look after herself," said Riley. "I say, Royden, is it true you kissed her? You're a brave man."

"A man is always said to have kissed a woman," said Roger gloomily, "if he's a gentleman. It's like divorce."

"Suppose," said Riley, "you give up being a gentleman and tell us what happened. I'm curious."

"I will not," said Roger. "How did you know?"

"Crowley saw you over the wall."

"Then you know fine what happened."

"Not necessarily," said Riley. "Crowley's no friend of yours."

"I'll knock his block off."

"Happy little party we've become," said Riley. "Our work looks like being a great success. I must mention in my report how we all worked together with the true team-spirit." He picked up, as if absent-mindedly, the remaining *tesserae* from the table and put them into his pocket. "Don't bother about these any more, Roger: I'll deal with them."

"Are you wise?" said Martin.

"I don't know, and I don't care, but that old goat is not going to get the better of me."

Roger emptied the handful of *tesserae* from his own pocket and handed them to Riley.

"I still want to go to London."

"No doubt. But you're in no mood to handle the matter of the mosaic. You go and chase your lady-love. I must say I'm glad you still prefer Dulcibella."

Roger blushed. "The trouble is, I don't know where to look for her. Certainly nobody here will give me her address."

"By the way," said Riley, "I wonder what's become of the children. If they were around, we'd hear them or see them. And where are that governess and tutor?"

"Perhaps," said Martin, "Mrs. Gale took them with her—the children, I mean, of course."

"Perhaps," said Riley, "the Professor—or Cornelia— or Miss Smith—have killed them and eaten them on toast."

"Hem!" coughed Roger.

Old Mrs. Gale stood in the doorway.

4

"Good morning, gentlemen," she said. "Nice of you to call. Do you want anything? Is there anybody you wish to see?"

"No thank you, ma'am," said Riley, recovering first. "We came to inquire after your health, if you please."

"I wondered," she said, "if you were from the school. I hope Henry is all right. He's not very strong. Isabella is much stronger."

"We are not from the school," said Riley. "But we are most interested to hear of your grandchildren. By the way, where *is* Henry?"

"Dulcibella arranged for them both to go to boarding schools. She took them there when she left. Henry is at— I forget the name." She looked round her. "I could get the address. It's in Sussex—they're both in Sussex—near Canterbury."

"Canterbury is in Kent, ma'am," said Martin.

"Is it?" She was not interested. "I know it's too far for any of us to visit them. But then, Dulcibella arranged that purposely. She left us in a rather unfriendly spirit. She never was one of the family. My poor son—" Her eyes widened as she noticed Roger. "Are you the young man—"

Riley cut in hastily: "No, ma'am. Mr. Royden has gone home. This is his twin brother: this is George."

Roger was obliged to answer to the name of "George" and bow.

"Your brother is a very wicked young man," said old Mrs. Gale. "He was, in a sense, responsible for my son's death. He brought a nasty poison into this house—and he was being far too familiar with my son's wife. I suppose," she added, eyeing them with keen suspicion, "your brother has gone after her—now that my son is dead?"

Roger said: "It's possible, ma'am. I am anxious to find him. We are worried about him."

"Disappeared," said Riley, shaking his head, "disappeared after the inquest."

"A guilty conscience," said old Mrs. Gale, "is a terrible scourge—or so it used to be in my young days. Conscience seems to be left out of the modern young men and young women."

"If," said Roger, "you could give me Mrs. Gale's address—"

"I am Mrs. Gale," said the old lady, drawing herself up.

"I beg your pardon: Mrs. Augustus Gale."

"She is not that any longer," snapped Augustus's mother.

"Mrs. Dulcibella Gale," said Roger, getting exasperated.

"Yes, I can tell you that: she asked to have her letters forwarded to—let me see."

She searched her memory while Roger fumed.

"No, I don't think she gave us an address," said old Mrs. Gale at last. "Ask the Professor. No, don't ask him; he is too absent-minded and forgetful. Ask Miss Smith: she knows everything. Is she still here? I don't know why she should be: there's no work for her now."

"She's here," said Riley. "She's with the Professor somewhere. She doesn't know Mrs. Dulcibella's whereabouts: we asked her. I mean, George asked her. You can't think how keen he is to find his brother."

Roger hoped Riley wouldn't overdo it: the old lady was no fool.

"I know," she said. "Get in touch with her solicitors: it's a London address. I can give you that. That was what she left us: she didn't trust us, you see. I'll go and get it. I have it in my desk." She waddled out, leaving them on tenterhooks.

5

While they were standing there waiting, and Riley was exasperating Roger by continuing to call him "George" while Martin tried clumsily to keep the peace, the door opened. Rupert entered, carrying a gun. Behind him was a tall, broad-shouldered man wearing a pea-soup-green suit.

"Hullo, chaps!" said Rupert. "You back again? I hear one of you swiped the bits of marble this morning. Good for you! But you'd better look out: my sister and old Nanny-goat will have your blood."

Riley stepped forward. "Don't worry: it's all arranged. By the way, I thought you hated shooting." He glanced down at the pair of rabbits dangling from Rupert's right hand; their muzzles dripped blood on to the pale carpet.

"Oh, I enjoy it fine now that Dad's not here to tell me to do it," said Rupert carelessly. He tossed the rabbits through the open door into the hall. "By the way, where *is* old Nanny-goat—do you know?"

"You mean the Professor?"

"Surely."

"He's out walking with Miss Smith," said Riley. "I think he's arranging for her new duties."

Rupert goggled. "I did see them in the distance as I came in," he said. "They had their heads close together. Do I get your meaning? Do you mean the old satyr has dropped my sister for that plain puss with the glasses?"

"Your sister has dropped him," said Riley, "and Miss Smith has caught him."

"Good for her!" said Rupert. "I always thought Cornelia must be off her head to let my father bully her into marrying that old sinner. In fact I offered to break his neck, or throw him down the steps—but she wouldn't agree." He leaned the gun against a chair, and threw himself on to a sofa. "God, what a change my father's departure has made in this place!" He glanced at the clock. "We ought to be just starting dinner." He remembered the stranger. "Come in, McGarten. These three gentlemen are archæologists. I forget their names. You'd better introduce yourselves. McGarten wants to see the Joan Farmer museum. Do you chaps know enough about it to show him round?" He said to McGarten: "They're really interested in some Roman mosaics."

McGarten bowed. "I come from the University of Ohio. There is great interest in Joan Farmer in the United States. I'm the great-great-nephew of James McGarten, who fought you in the War of Independence." He bowed again as if to indicate that so far as he was concerned this little matter was forgiven and forgotten. "In fact, I believe my ancestor once met Joan Farmer's husband, who was an actor called Owen. Anyway, in my family we have several Farmer relics, and we had some idea of presenting one of these to your museum here. But I understand that the owner, Augustus Gale, has just died."

"Take him down to the museum," said Rupert, "and show him what we've got. I'll go and get my grandmother. She's the owner of the house now, and she's the one to whom you should give the relic. Don't," he said to McGarten, "whatever you do, give it to that old chap with the white beard."

He explained to Riley: "It's a gold cross set with diamonds, a tribute to Joan Farmer from some admirer. Bose would pretend to be 'examining' it and we'd never see it again. Don't give it to Cornelia, either. She's got a 'thing' about Joan Farmer: she'd probably get rid of it in some way." As Riley led McGarten to the door, Rupert called after them: "Take him to the museum, and then if you like to the Joan Farmer site outside. I'll rustle up drinks for you by the time you come back." He hauled on the bell-rope and yelled: "Robert! Blast that fellow, there's no discipline in this house now. If he comes, tell him to bring drinks—I'll go and get Granny." He left.

6

Old Mrs. Gale returned carrying a piece of paper. She handed it to Roger.

"Here you are, young man."

"Thank you."

"You're welcome. Of course, I know who you are. That rascally Irishman didn't deceive me for a moment. Twin brother George, indeed! Does he think I'm in my dotage?" She smiled. "Don't be alarmed: I know it was just his joke. One can forgive an Irishman anything." There was a pause.

"I hope," said Roger, deeply embarrassed, "you don't really think I had anything to do with the death of your son, except by accident?"

"I know you didn't, young man. You see, I know the real culprit."

"You do?"

"Myself. I should never have told him—about you and Dulcibella. It was very wrong of me and I'm paying for it."

"I'm sorry," was all Roger could think of to say.

Mrs. Gale gave him a sharp look, seemed about to say more, and then changed the subject.

"Who was that man I saw coming in with Rupert just now?"

"An American. He has come to see the Joan Farmer museum. His name is McGarten."

"Ah. Our lives will be unbearable henceforth—especially when we begin charging a fee as Professor Bose wishes. By the way, where is the Professor? He should be showing the visitor around: we don't want strangers let loose alone in the museum. They may take something: we've had a theft there already, I'm told. Cornelia said something about it."

"Don't worry, ma'am," said Roger. "The American has come to give *you* something, not to take anything away."

"Give *me* something," said Mrs. Gale, looking sharply suspicious.

"A relic for the museum: a Joan Farmer relic—a gold cross set with diamonds, I gather."

"I don't want it. I hate the whole thing. I wish we'd never come here. My son was as mad in pursuit of this dead woman as if she'd been alive. I've often heard him speak of a gold cross set with diamonds: he knew it was in America and he wanted at one time to go over there and try to get it back. Fortunately he couldn't afford the journey. Where's the young man? We must offer him something to eat. Where's that Mr. Riley? I want to tell him something—something that will please him. I have come to a decision—an important decision." She sounded excited.

"I think your grandson has gone to see about some refreshment," said Roger. "McGarten will be back presently. Riley is with him. It'll be all right. Do sit down, ma'am, and don't agitate yourself."

Old Mrs. Gale sat down with a sigh.

"At my age, it's hard to suffer such a blow. I'm afraid I shall have to leave here. I don't wish to stay now that Augustus is gone—and the children are gone, too. Professor Bose will be glad to get rid of me and have full charge. Cornelia, it seems, doesn't want to marry him. I shall take her with me if she'll come. We'll go and live in some brighter spot, on the south coast: Bournemouth, perhaps. Somewhere gay, removed from the past. I am tired of the past. At my age, when one has so little future to look forward to, one has no time to spare for contemplating anything but the present. My own past, perhaps, but not this Joan Farmer's. That reminds me: I mean to arrange through the lawyers that your archæological expedition shall have access to the piece of Roman mosaic that lies inside our boundary wall."

"You do?" said Roger and Martin together.

"I could never quite see my son's point of view. But he was obstinate about some things. It was that hillock— the wretched hillock on which was the summer-house where that woman wrote her plays."

"We shall try to preserve the hillock," said Martin eagerly. "We don't wish—we never have wished—to damage anything."

"You'd do better," said old Mrs. Gale, "to get rid of it. It's nothing but a nuisance and always has been. After all, we can't always be preserving something where somebody has done something, can we? If we did, there'd be no progress. Still, I shouldn't say anything about it yet if I were you." She leaned towards them confidentially. "I'll see to it: I'll tell Mr. Riley. The Professor will be angry, but I'm not dead yet. I think I'll stay here after all, just to annoy him."

Rupert entered, followed by Robert, carrying a larger tray.

"Oh, there you are, Grandma—at the receipt of custom. Good. Not tea this time!" he said to the others. "Aren't they back yet?"

At that moment there were sounds outside. McGarten and Riley burst into the room. They looked scared.

"Something happened?" said Rupert coolly.

"In the museum! The portrait!" gasped McGarten. He led the way out. Riley said quietly to old Mrs. Gale:

"Don't disturb yourself, ma'am. The portrait of Joan Farmer is a little damaged. I think it can be repaired." He turned to Roger and Martin. "It's curious. Come and have a look."

They all went except Rupert and Mrs. Gale.

7

It was McGarten who led the way to the museum, he who pointed out the damage.

"Look there: somebody has climbed up and made an incision."

They looked. The incision was across the mouth; it had been carefully done, and the canvas had been turned back so that the effect was of a grin showing projecting teeth: it was horrible.

"Nasty bit of work," said Riley.

The portrait hung on the wall at the end of the gallery. It was full length and not far short of life size; it hung from a picture-rail, and the base of the frame reached the floor. McGarten took his stand beside it; his head was a little above that of the woman in the picture.

"I won't touch it," he said, "though I long to restore the original expression."

"You know it!" said Riley.

"Everyone all over the world knows this portrait of Joan Farmer," said McGarten reverently. "It is the only one in existence, so far as we know: painted five or six years before she died, when she was in her prime." He bent forward as if to look at some detail, and laid his hand on the side of the frame. The picture moved.

"One moment," said Roger. He walked to the picture, moved it outward a little more, and looked behind it. He emerged looking red and flustered.

"This is a police matter, of course," said McGarten. "Have we any check on visitors?"

"I think," said Riley, "you are the first outside visitor; the house isn't open yet to visitors. I don't think anyone but members of the family have been here lately."

"And yourselves."

"We have not left the drawing-room. Some member of the family has been with us all the time. We must leave it to old Mrs. Gale to decide whether she'll call in the police. I don't think she will; they've only just left. I expect she's had enough of them."

McGarten examined the cut with a pocket magnifying glass.

"This has been recently done." He turned to Roger. "Did you see anything from behind?"

"No," said Roger shiftily. Riley and Martin were astonished that McGarten accepted his answer.

McGarten said: "It's to be hoped that the old lady will get expert advice in at once. Also she ought to find out if she has any servants with grudges. It's difficult to see any purpose except malice. She'd better keep the room locked up from now on."

"Let's go and tell her," said Riley. "Or rather, I'll tell her: she quite likes me."

As they left, Roger glanced back as he had done on their previous visit. But now the face of the portrait wore not a look of sadness as if of grief at their going, but an evil grin.

He went out and closed the door quickly.

8

When they got back to the hotel, Riley said to Roger:

"What did you find?"

"This," said Roger. He drew from his pocket and held out on the palm of his hand a small pink tablet.

"Is it—?" said Riley.

"I think it's one of my mercury biniodide tablets."

"Then Augustus didn't take it?"

"I don't know. I wish I'd counted the things. The police took my case."

The hall porter came up.

"A police constable left this for you, sir."

It was the so-called first-aid case. It was covered with fingerprint powder. Roger tried the clasp: the case was locked.

"Come upstairs," he said. "I've got my key."

Riley and Martin watched as he opened the case. Inside was a cardboard box containing a row of bottles. The poison label was conspicuous among them. Roger shook the pink tablets on to the palm of his hand.

"Twenty-three," he said. "There should be twenty-five."

"Then Augustus took one," said Riley, "and some maniac popped the other into the slit in the portrait where Joan Farmer's mouth was."

Martin spoke last. "I think," he said ponderously, "the maniac and the person who poisoned Augustus are one and the same." He turned to Roger. "What are you going to do about it?"

"Nothing," said Roger. "I'm leaving for London at once."

"There's no train," said Riley.

"On my Vespa."

"Heavens!" said Riley. "A hundred and thirty miles on a Vespa! That's love."

"Oh, go and dig a hole," said Roger, "and fall in!"

"We're starting tomorrow morning," said Riley, "on *this* side of the wall. I've made a hit with the old lady. Good luck to you with the young one! When will you be back—if ever?"

"I don't know."

IX

When Roger found Dulcibella, she was sitting at a table in the dining-room of a London hotel. She looked exactly as she had done when he had first seen her, and she moved him in exactly the same way.

Afterwards, over coffee and Benedictine, they talked.

He told her all that had happened since the inquest. He was then going on to discuss their future together. She stopped him.

"Roger, dear," she said, "I think the time has now come to tell you the truth."

He gazed at her in dismay, knowing that he was about to hear something intensely unpleasant. She said in low tones:

"Augustus did not commit suicide."

"What do you mean?" Horror gripped him. She smiled.

"No, it wasn't I who put one of your poison tablets into his tea. I am not capable of that. Besides, I didn't hate Augustus enough to wish to kill him—so horribly."

"You mean—somebody did?"

She acquiesced.

"And you know who it was?"

Again she acquiesced. "But I shall never say so to any living soul but you. And you are not to repeat what I say—for your own sake. No one would believe you. They might even suspect you. Many people did at the time. I might have myself if I hadn't known the truth."

"People really suspected me?"

"Of course."

"Why 'of course'? Martin said so, but I thought he was just being Martin—over-cautious."

"They thought you had the best motive," she said with a slight smile.

"But that! How ghastly! As if I would—"

"Would you in no circumstances have got rid of Augustus?"

"No."

"Not even to get *me*?"

"No."

"You are a poor lover."

"I am not. One doesn't kill—certainly not with poison."

"No. But would you never have wanted to get rid of Augustus—in your heart?"

"I suppose so. I never thought of it in that way."

"I oughtn't to have said I would have suspected you, Roger, if I hadn't known the truth. One could never suspect you of such an action, at such a speed." With a change of tone she went on: "So somebody did for poor Joan Farmer after all. She had it coming to her, didn't she?"

"I don't understand."

"Don't you understand—haven't you the imagination to real-ise—that Augustus's passion for Joan Farmer made everyone hate her?"

"Even though she's been dead for over a century?"

"Even more, for that very reason. Who can fight a dead woman? Don't you realise that there were three women in that house who were jealous of her? His mother, Cornelia and myself. You know, Roger"—she laid one of her beautiful white hands on his knee—"we were all fond of Augustus in our way. You never saw him at his best, but he had charm. He charmed me into marrying him. His mother naturally adored him—though she found him madly irritating at times. Cornelia would have liked to take her mother's place. But she never could—not because of me, but because of Joan Farmer."

"I see," said Roger, though he didn't. He could see no charm in Augustus Gale.

"Even that plain little secretary had a crush on him," said Dulcie with a soft, cruel laugh. "She used to work for him far into the night, typing and copying notes and looking up references in books. Her eyes were red, from over-strain and weeping. He could make her cry. He liked to make her cry. When we were first married, he liked to make *me* cry."

"Damn!" said Roger.

"That ceased to be possible after the birth of my first child. The second one was not conceived in love but in duty—my duty, not to Augustus, but to Henry. I had to provide a brother or a sister for Henry. I don't believe in only children. Augustus was an only child. But neither wife nor children nor anything else could cure Augustus of Joan Farmer."

"What part did Professor Bose play in all this? Cornelia accused him of encouraging Augustus in his obsession."

"I don't know. Bose is just a silly old man with an axe to grind. I doubt if he had much influence with Augustus. My impression was that Augustus was using Bose— making use of him in the service of Joan Farmer." She laughed. "So funny to think of Bose and Miss Smith together! She'll kill him! She's one of those apparently meek women who need a tyrant to keep them in order. She will despise Bose once he has married her."

She stopped. Roger waited. He did not like to ask Dulcie a direct question about Augustus's death, yet he burned to know what she knew. In the end he said:

"Why did Cornelia say all that? She accused me, too, you know." He had not thought it honourable to tell Dulcibella that Cornelia had kissed him.

"Can't you guess?" said Dulcie, turning to look at him with very serious gaze. "Think, Roger: put the facts together—the facts you know. You're an archæologist: you're supposed to be able to do that and draw correct conclusions. People are always likening you archæologists to detectives."

Roger thought. His mind became blank because he was thinking about Dulcibella, trying to read her mind, and suffering from the emotions due to contiguity.

"To which two women did you show the contents of your case? Who poured out the tea that evening at my request? Who suffered most from Augustus's determination to sacrifice everybody to his passion for the dead?"

Roger thought again. He saw it all: the case, Cornelia beside him in his room, the badinage that occurred as he opened the cases before Dulcie entered; the drawing-room with the huge crystal chandelier, the tea-table—he did not clearly remember who presided at the tea-table, though he did remember that Dulcibella was not doing so; she was near him while he was being taught to play some idiotic card game. The rest was a blur except for the seizure and exit of Augustus, and his own departure to get a doctor.

He said to himself: "She *was* wearing gloves—white gloves. All the ladies were wearing long gloves. It was part of the show."

"I beg your pardon?" said Dulcibella. "We had to wear gloves: that was one of Augustus's orders."

"There were no fingerprints on the case or the bottle," said Roger, "except mine." He thought again for a while. "Was it she who damaged the picture?"

"It's just the kind of thing she would do," said Dulcibella. "And the poison tablet behind the picture confirms it—doesn't it?"

"She must be raving mad."

"Not *raving* mad—just mad," said Dulcibella.

"Oughtn't we to do something about it, for the sake of the others?"

"Why? Who is there she can harm? She won't want to hurt anybody now she has, as she thinks, poisoned Joan Farmer. *I'm* not there, nor are my children, and I shall never go back. But even if I did she wouldn't bother with me: I was never her enemy. I was her friend."

"I know. She said *that* herself. She seemed to know you'd tried to arrange for her to get a husband. She didn't take at all to poor old Martin, by the way."

"I know," said Dulcie calmly. "She fell in love with *you*. That was obvious from the start."

"You know?" There seemed no reason why he should now conceal from her the attack made on him by Cornelia.

"That was perhaps the chief motive for her getting rid of Augustus," said Dulcibella. "He was determined that she should marry old Bose. So at one stroke she got rid of him, and of me— her rival."

"She killed her *father?*"

Dulcibella surveyed him. "My dear Roger, don't you know that a girl can hate her father more violently than she hates anyone if he, her natural protector, turns out to be a menace in some way? Oh no, of course, you are a chemist, not a psychologist. Don't worry about Cornelia: she'll be a good girl for the rest of her life now. She will harm no one, she will be kind to the poor, and in the end she will forget the whole incident: she will even deny it to herself. You have no idea of the powers of oblivion possessed by the human mind." She got up. "Excuse me, Roger, but I must go and pack."

"Pack!"

"Yes: my plane leaves tomorrow at ten."

"Your plane? You are going abroad?"

"I am going to the United States of America. I have an invitation from the McGarten family. They are very rich and very much interested in the Joan Farmer story."

"But I thought you hated the Joan Farmer story?"

"These people will never become obsessed with the past: they're too much alive—too busy with the present. By the way, I've met Homer McGarten: he'll be travelling back with me tomorrow."

"Then you know all about the portrait?"

"Yes, Roger, but I wanted to see you, to hear you tell the story, and to say goodbye to you."

"Then it's goodbye?"

"Yes. Just an episode in your career as an archæologist. Don't look so hurt! I like you; for a brief while I thought I could love you. You are so young, and there has been so little youth in my life. But being married to Augustus has perhaps aged me. I don't find youth as attractive as I did, except in small doses. And there are the children: you didn't want the children, and who could blame you?"

He pleaded with her, knowing that it was no use: that he had already accepted her decision.

"And Roger," she said finally, "it wouldn't do, you know. If I married you, you'd be ruined, and so would I. They'd say we got rid of Augustus between us: a *crime passionel*, and it wouldn't have been forgiven us as the means was poison. They'd say you supplied the poison and I used it. Everybody would have forgotten that it wasn't I who performed the tea-ceremony that evening."

"Martin said something like that."

"Martin is your very good friend. Go back to him. Go back to the party and help to dig out those Muses. I hear Grandma is on your side: she has fallen for that attractive red-haired Irishman. What vitality these Gales have for better or worse! I wonder how my own children will turn out. I hope their schools won't destroy all their individuality."

With a final pat she left him.

He stayed for a long time where she left him. She had not done him justice. He was much more hurt than she knew.

2

Time passed. He did not forget, but he put this episode away in a separate compartment of his mind, so that he could lead his life in a normal and comfortable manner. He did not go back to Geffrye House and the party finished the dig without him.

Old Mrs. Gale lived to be one hundred and two. She survived Professor Bose by two years and in the end she reigned supreme, over Joan Farmer and the Muses. Cornelia lived with her, and as Dulcibella predicted, became pious and an indefatigable social worker. She did not marry.

Many visitors came to see the remains. They gave the mosaics cursory attention, and the Joan Farmer monument—which had been built on the hillock from subscriptions collected by the Joan Farmer Society—did not interest them greatly, because few of them knew who she was and none of them had read a word she had written. They left their tribute in the form, not of wreaths, but of ice-cream- and cigarette-cartons round the base of the hillock. One of Robert Brook's jobs was to collect these remains after the visit of every party. The visitors then went back to the town of Siccard to enjoy themselves at the new Fun Fair on the shore.

3

In the summer after her grandmother's death, Cornelia was killed. She was struck down by a car outside the gates of Geffrye House.

Opinions differed regarding what happened. At the inquest, one witness said she stepped into the road without looking round, in an absent-minded way; the driver said she threw herself under the wheels. The verdict was "death by misadventure".

She was by now well known in Siccard for her charities and her oddities. She was a tall, slim figure always dressed in black, and many said she must have been handsome in her youth; she still had brilliant blue eyes. All agreed, however, that she was a little queer in the head, and some remembered the death of her father, twenty years before. She had had a tragic life, they said: first her father's death, then years of self-sacrifice in looking after her grandmother, and some hinted at a disappointment in love. Her father had been a very strange man, to put it mildly, and no doubt she inherited some of his queerness, poor woman.

Cornelia was the last of the Gales: the name died with her. Rupert had been killed in Australia in an aeroplane crash; he left three daughters who married young. Henry and Isabella changed their name when their mother remarried. Dulcibella married a rich American who met her at the McGartens: he adored her and fulfilled her slightest wish, and she was very happy.

Milton Keynes UK
Ingram Content Group UK Ltd.
UKHW050458280324
440101UK00017B/1281